Mr. Lincoln's Gold

By   Norris Caldwell

This book is a work of fiction. Places, events, and situations in this story are purely fictional. Any resemblance to actual persons, living or dead, is coincidental.

ISBN: 1-4107-3811-6 (e-book)
ISBN: 1-4107-3810-8 (Paperback)
ISBN: 1-4107-3809-4 (Dust Jacket)

Library of Congress Control Number: 2003091902

This book is printed on acid free paper.

Printed in the United States of America
Bloomington, IN

1stBooks – rev. 03/29/03

Chapter 1

I didn't want to be the only coward in Wayne County, Illinois. I enlisted in the Union Army on January 8th, 1862, three weeks after my eighteenth birthday. Charley Rogers' uncle was getting a group of Illinois boys together to form a brigade and join General U.S. Grant at Cairo. General Grant had just captured the port town of Paducah, Kentucky and word was he was going to head down the Mississippi and then on to the Tennessee. I guess if I had to fight in the war, I might as well ride on a boat as far south as I could.

Colonel Rogers, Charley's uncle, served with General Grant in the Mexican war when Grant was a captain. Mr. Rogers said if he had to go to war he would rather fight with Grant than any other man on earth.

My name is Marcus Wade. I grew up on a small farm outside Galena. I wish I could say I had a happy upbringing but that just isn't the way it was. My momma and daddy were always fussing with each other and by the time I was eight, all my three older brothers and one sister had already left home. Sara, my sister, told me I needed to leave home too or I'd never live to be a grown man. My daddy was just plain mean. I never heard him say a kind word to my momma, and he would beat me with his razor strop for nothing more than spilling some milk on the table. One night after he had been drinking I thought he was going to kill me. He hung me on the big beam in the barn with a plow rope and said he would leave me there until I learned to act like a man. I didn't even know what I had done to make him so mad. He wrapped the plow rope around my arms and I couldn't move. He would hit me on my back and butt with his belt and then go off and sleep awhile. When he woke up he would come back and hit me some more. I guess he would have let me die hanging there, but momma came out and cut me down. She told me we were going to grandpa and mammaw's house, and she was going to leave me there until daddy cooled down. That was when I was twelve and from that night on I only saw my daddy about three or

1

four more times. I stayed with grandpa and mammaw until I graduated from Galena High School in the summer of 1861.

Things were better at my grandparent's house. They were poor people and I had to work awfully hard to help keep things going, but at least I was away from my daddy. At first I would see momma about once a month when she would bring some chickens and vegetables over to grandpa's house. I think momma loved me, but she was so scared of daddy she finally got to where she didn't even hug me when she came. Finally, she quit coming all together.

Although I had no stomach for war and fighting, I can't say I was too sorry to leave home. Most any life at all would be better than what I had. Charley Rogers had been my one true friend and I knew Charley and me would make it fine as long as we could stay in the same outfit.

I learned to shoot a rifle when I was thirteen. Grandpa had an old flintlock that worked most of the time. I got to where I could hit a rabbit fifty yards away. Once I killed a pheasant as it rose up out of the sage field. I knew I wouldn't have any trouble learning to shoot the new Springfield rifled musket the army was issuing the boys. My problem was, would I be able to aim it at another American boy and actually shoot at him?

I hadn't thought too much about the war and why we were fighting the Rebs anyway. My teacher in the twelfth grade said a lot of the southern farms had black slaves on them and Mr. Lincoln wanted us to go down there and set the slaves free. I figured slaves might be better off living where they had a place to sleep and food to eat, but I guess it really wasn't right for one man to actually own another man.

I always thought of myself as a good American, but I hadn't convinced myself that we had much right going down to other American's homes and shooting at them just because they thought differently about things than we did.   I met a boy from Mississippi one day at school who was visiting his aunt. As I looked at the boy from Mississippi I remember he looked like all the other tenth graders in the room.   He was quite well spoken and polite, and although he said his words with a funny twang, I was somewhat impressed by him. I thought of that Mississippi boy as I loaded my gear on the big boat at Cairo. What would I say to that boy if I had to point a Springfield .58 Caliber rifle at him and shoot him dead? I guess this is what had bothered me ever since we started our training in the regiment back in Galena.

Charley's uncle and all the other officers in the regiment had drilled into us the thought that the Rebs were our mortal enemies, and we should be prepared to kill any and all we came in contact with. Lieutenant Ames was especially hateful toward the southerners. He painted bearded faces on stuffed bags made to look like gray clad southern soldiers. During our training, he would have us drive our bayonets into the dummies and yell "Go to Hell, Reb!" as we removed our bayonets and went on to the next dummy. It made me sick to my stomach. That Reb hadn't done anything to hurt the people in Illinois, and he certainly hadn't done anything to me. As I found my place on the boat leaving Cairo I knew I had no business in Mr. Lincoln's army.

Chapter 2

As I stood on the moving ship I looked in both directions and counted nine transport vessels like the one I was on and four boats whose sides were covered with iron. Eight cannons were mounted on each of the ironclads, four on each side. Closely behind the iron vessels were three huge wooden ships of war. Sixteen cannons lined each side of these massive ships. I didn't know there were that many ships in the whole Union Navy. Charley's uncle, Colonel Rogers, told us there were over 20,000 Union soldiers on the ships and he didn't know how many Navy men.

I never saw General Grant. Charley said he heard he was on one of the larger war ships.

On February the tenth we unloaded three miles below Fort Henry, a Confederate held encampment about sixty miles below Paducah, Kentucky. I almost lost my breakfast as I thought of charging up to the fort in the face of blazing cannon and Rebel soldiers firing muskets at us. My initial fear was unfounded. We never fired a shot at Fort Henry. The gunboats bombarded the fort relentlessly for two days, and by the time we reached the fort, the Confederates were all gone. We heard they all escaped to Fort Donelson.

It took our large force several hours to walk the twelve miles from Ft. Henry to Fort Donelson. It was unseasonably warm for February, and the men all shed their heavy coats and blankets and left them with the commissary wagons at Fort Henry. It would be a mistake that would almost kill us all. It was February 12, Mr. Lincoln's birthday. After setting up our defenses in a arc three miles wide around the fort, we prepared for battle the next day. During the night the weather changed drastically. It first started raining, then at midnight it changed to sleet. By dawn a full gale was driving snow on top of freezing men on both sides. The southerners were as ill prepared as our boys, and by the time we overtook the fort we found wounded Reb soldiers frozen to death where they sat. It was a miserable sight. The Rebs put up a gallant fight but they were too lightly provisioned and were outnumbered two to one. The commanding officer of the fort surrendered his command to General Grant at noon on the thirteenth. I fired my rifle one time and I feel sure it was of no great help in the victory. I was too cold and hungry to worry about who won and who lost. I never knew what happened to the southern boys inside the fort. I suppose General Grant left a few of our men there to keep them at bay but I can`t say for sure. It would have suited me fine if he had asked me to ride out the war sitting there on the Tennessee river in a dry fort talking to the enemy boys.

It took us a good ten hours to walk back to the boats and get loaded up. The commissary wagons got all mixed up and delivered the wrong coats to the wrong boats. We had to take whatever coat and blanket we could get. I got a pretty good deal out of the swap. The coat I got had a full package of real coffee in one pocket and a big bag of cooked peanuts in the other. Some yank was going to be pretty mad that night when he couldn`t find his coffee and peanuts.

We rode in the boats for several weeks and I was getting pretty butt weary.

Although I hated the walk back at the Fort Donelson battle I was really ready to get off that boat. Everything on the boat was crowded. There was plenty of food, but it took over two hours to get through the line to pick up our rations. By the time I got back to my gear the food that had been hot was already cold. I drank a lot of coffee but there was no way to keep it hot there on the ship. I folded up what was left of my coffee stash and decided to wait until we got off the boats to try and cook it. Charley and I ate the peanuts and they were pretty good. The cooks on the boat made big, thick biscuits and they were tasty even when they were cold.

General Grant finally let us take a break from the boats. We unloaded north of a town called Savannah on the banks of the Tennessee River. The weather had gotten a lot better in mid March.

We set up our tents according to regiments. All our boys were from the same county in Illinois but the men in the next company were from Ohio. After several hours of close order drills we were allowed to take a break and visit with the Ohio boys. It was funny to see how different they were in some ways, yet so like us in others. All the Ohio boys had let their beards grow and they looked much older than our bunch. Colonel Rogers required that we shave every other day. He said he wanted us to look sharp when we went into battle for our country.

With my upbringing I hadn't been around a lot of boys my own age. There were six boys and three girls in my graduating class at Galena High School, and other than Charley, I really hadn't been close to any of them. I always had to go straight home from school and do chores and take care of things around grandpa's house. I didn't know much about how other boys lived. When one of the Ohio boys pulled out a bottle of his daddy's homemade whiskey I was reluctant to take a drink. All I knew about whiskey was what it did to my daddy and how mean it made him act. The Ohio bunch kidded me a lot but I still wouldn't taste the whiskey. Charley took a big swig and I thought his eyes were going to pop out. He told me he and Bertha Jo Jackson got tight on her daddy's homebrew one night, but I kinda doubt it. I could tell right off that Charley wasn't a drinker of spirits and probably never would be.

I really enjoyed the Ohio boys company. After a while I realized that although we were from different states we were pretty much the same inside. Before I went to bed that night I thought again of the boy from Mississippi I had met in school back in the tenth grade. I felt if I could sit down and talk to him like I had just done with the Ohio boys, we could somehow become friends. I knew that night I could never kill another American boy. It was something I was going to have to handle and I wasn't sure how I would do it.

I had never been much of a church goer. It wasn't because I didn't want to go but Sunday was just like other days around the house and chores had to be done. When I was nine, mammaw explained to me about Jesus, and I think after we prayed together I became a believer. I didn't pray every night but on this night I felt the need. I asked Jesus to be with me and protect me, but especially, I asked him to keep all the southern boys away from me in battle so I wouldn't have to shoot at them. This one thought was haunting me every day as I felt us drawing closer to battle.

Chapter 3

We relaxed in the camp at Savannah all the month of March and by April 1ˢᵗ the weather was so nice you could actually see dogwoods blooming on the edges of the woods. The boys were in top shape. Everyone had their rifles clean and in good order and our extra change of clothes was neatly packed in our backpacks. We knew we were going to move when the commissary wagons came by and passed out traveling rations of hardtack, beans and salt pork. On April 2ⁿᵈ Lieutenant Ames told us to prepare for a march south toward Corinth, Mississippi. We were through with our boat rides and from now on we would be on foot. I think most of the boys were glad to be free of the confinement of the boats although the thought of walking for the next several hundred miles was not a pleasant one. We filled our canteens with fresh water and broke camp.

I rather enjoyed the walk south. The land was hospitable and not too hilly. We were on the west side of the Tennessee and ever so often we could see the river below us. We had not seen a Reb since Fort Donelson and most of us had never actually looked eye to eye with an armed opponent. I can`t explain it but I knew in my heart that somewhere south of us harm was waiting.

We camped just above the river where supply boats had brought food, fresh water and summer weight shirts for us. The spot was called Pittsburg Landing. After mess call on the evening of the 5ᵗʰ, Charley and I met up with a couple of the Ohio boys we got to know and walked over to the ridge overlooking the Tennessee river. We could see one of the supply boats pulling out from Pittsburg Landing and for a few minutes no one said a word. The sight was breathtaking. If there was a prettier place on God`s earth than this, I knew I would never see it. It was worth the cramped boat ride and the long marches to be able to sit at this spot and simply enjoy life. All the boys were eating fresh apples the boat had delivered. We were looking up at hundreds of bright stars when Quint, one of the Ohio regulars broke the silence.

"How could anyone be thinking about war on a night like this?" Quint said. "Maybe Johnny Reb isn't anywhere within five hundred miles of this beautiful place."

We didn't say anything, but we knew that somewhere out there in the wilderness there were southern boys looking at the same sky we were looking at. Very soon these two groups would have to meet.

We didn't know it at the time, but less than two miles southwest of us a large group of Confederate soldiers was waiting to attack our encampments. General Albert Sydney Johnston had force marched his entire army of 40,000 troops the twenty five miles from Corinth to meet the advancing Union Army he knew was moving south. General Johnston felt that a surprise attack on the Yankee forces would serve him better than trying to defend the rail center at Corinth. General Grant joined with other foot soldiers in the region and had 37,000 troops at his disposal with an additional 20,000 under the command on General Don Carlos Buell moving by boat from Savannah.

Our regiment had been assigned to General Sherman's division on the western most section of the area. There was a well used dirt road running north and south. About two hundred yards from our tents was a little wooden church. On the morning of the 6th of April Charley and me strolled down to the church to take a look. We had just finished breakfast and our Springfield's were safely stacked outside our tents. Of all the mornings on our march this was the prettiest. We had hoped to get a glimpse of General Sherman but a picket guarding the western side of the road said Sherman and his entire staff were having breakfast with General Grant over on the bluff by the river. It's funny about the Generals. I have been in Mr. Lincoln's army now for three months and I haven't actually laid eyes on a real live General.

As we got to the little church we noticed a crude sign hanging over the door post. It simply said , *Shiloh.* I didn't know where the name came from but figured it must have something to do with a place in the Bible. Our sergeant told us we could have about an hour before we would have close order drill and inspection of our rifles. Charley sat in one of the benches in the little church and just stared ahead. This was the first building we had been in since February. I was looking at one of the song books in a rack behind one of the benches. I opened the book and my eyes fell on page 78 and the song, "It is Well With My Soul." I read the first verse;

"When peace, like a river, attendeth my way, When sorrows like sea billows roll; whatever my lot, Thou hast taught me to say, It is Well, it is Well with my soul."

I looked up at a picture of Jesus holding a small child in his lap. There was an eerie quiet about the place. I can't explain it but I had a feeling I would never know this feeling again.

Charley jumped to his feet when we heard the first blast from cannon fire. It sounded like it was right outside the church. We wondered what our artillery boys were doing practicing this early in the morning, so we left the church and looked outside. Men were running everywhere, most in just their underwear tops, some grabbing their britches and hurriedly pulling them on as they ran. We started toward our tent to grab our rifles when a cannon ball exploded not ten feet from Charley. When I saw Charley go down, I could see that the right side of his skull was blown off. Half of Charley's brains were in what was left of his head and the other half was on the ground by Charley's lifeless body . In front of me I saw hundreds of boys in gray charging our positions and yelling like crazy. My only hope was to head back toward the church. In front of me was certain death.

As I looked around to try to find a gun I saw a dead sergeant lying face down. I picked up his Springfield. It fell apart in my hands. Whatever hit the sergeant had torn the gun in half. Instinctively I grabbed the bayonet off the gun and ran to the church. Smoke was everywhere. The smell was a combination of gunpowder and human flesh. I never saw any of our boys fire a shot. They were all running toward the river. I remember thinking this was the end of the world. The noise, the confusion, the total lack of order and the smoke and fire was consuming me.

I dove under the church and peered out in all directions. The Rebs had all crossed the road and there didn't seem to be any boys in gray on the western side. They were all running toward our main force by the river. I saw hundreds of our boys fall under the Rebs relentless fire but I never saw a single Reb even get wounded. At this rate the battle would be over in a few hours.

I saw one of the supply wagons coming full speed up the road toward the church. Just as I yelled at the two yanks holding the reins of the two horses, a cannon shell hit in a big oak tree right above the wagon. The flying metal and tree limbs tore into the two doomed soldiers and drove them to the ground. They were both dead before they hit solid earth. The blast startled the horses and they stopped in their tracks. The terrified horses tossed their heads from side to side as if trying to disengage from their harnesses. I knew this would be the only chance I would have to stay alive. I ran to the wagon, jumped in the seat and grabbed the lead rein. I urged the horses forward. They were headed south and I didn`t try to change them. All I wanted to do was get away from this spot as fast as I could. I figured all my brigade was dead anyway and I was weary of this war. I didn`t know where I was going but I knew I had to vacate this land. We had invaded the domain of these Rebs and they were Hell bent on stopping us right here. From what I could see they had done their job quite well.

I was well versed in handling a two team rig and by twenty paces I had the horses at full gallop. We ran into skirmishes at every sector and the results appeared to be the same everywhere. The Rebs had mounted a devastating attack that was obviously well planned. We had heard rumors of General Sydney Johnston and it appeared that everything we heard was true. I could see no way that our boys in blue could stop this endless horde of gray clad warriors.

I must have traveled five miles before I cleared the battle area. The road forked and I guided the horses toward the river. Maybe one of our boats was there to pick up stragglers and take us to safety. I stopped at an incline where a path led to the water. I saw no boats and no human beings. A racoon and her small family was lazily getting a drink of water, not caring that just north of her men were dying in great numbers.

I disembarked the wagon and stared toward the noise of the battle. The roar of cannon was still an ever constant reminder of what I had recently seen. I knew each burst of the heavy guns was sending death and destruction toward our boys. Occasionally I could hear the sound of larger guns. I assumed these were our twelve pounders answering the Reb`s fire. I wondered what General Grant and

General Sherman were doing. Were they dead? Had they surrendered? Was the gallant effort of the Army of Illinois over?

I thought of Charley. Days of our childhood flashed before me. I could see Charley swinging out on the rope from the hay loft of the barn, laughing and daring me to join him. I could almost touch Charley as I thought of the carefree afternoons when we would sneak to Mason's Creek and skinny dip in the frigid water. Was Charley really dead? Had I just dreamed the last two hours? Could I get in the wagon and ride back up the road and find Charley smiling and joking with the other boys in our regiment? As the guns continued to roar I knew this was certainly no dream. What I had seen was real and I doubt the ages had ever produced a more devastating day than what I had just witnessed.

I sat on a large stone by the water and thought of my situation. Was I a coward? Had I become a deserter? I hadn't had time to think of such things. If I hadn't jumped in the wagon I would be like Charley, dead on the ground up by Shiloh Church. What was I to do now? I was convinced the Rebs would win the battle and capture the boys not killed on the spot. I was through with war, but I didn't want to go to a southern prison.

All of a sudden I was quite thirsty and hungry. I bent over and got a good drink of the pure river water and walked to the wagon to see if any provisions were to be found. I threw back the canvas covering the opening at the rear of the wagon and noticed several wooden trunks lining the bottom of the wagon. None were stacked on the others and they appeared to be substantially made with iron hasps attached to the iron bands surrounding the wood frames of the boxes. The box nearest the driver's seat had been opened for the lock was loosely hanging in the hasp. Hoping I would find food, I removed the hasp and opened the trunk. What I saw caused me to ease to a sitting position on the next box. Lined in perfect order were rectangle boxes full of gold coins. I lifted one of the boxes and saw it contained $10 Gold Eagles. I estimated there were a hundred coins in each box. I figured the large trunk had at least fifty of these smaller cartons. I had been pretty good at ciphering in school, and it didn't take me long to realize that the trunk I was looking in had around $50,000 in U.S. gold stacked neatly in the smaller boxes. The trunk was almost too heavy for me to move, but as I turned it to the side I could see the mark, $10.00 U. S. Gold, written on the end in white paint. I counted ten of the large trunks with the ten dollar mark and six marked $1. I took the crowbar laying on the floor of the wagon and pried off the hasp of one of the trunks holding the one dollar coins. The coins were much smaller and each small box had at least five hundred of the one dollar coins.

I realized what I had come upon. This was the pay wagon for Grant's entire army. When we joined up we were promised $13 a month for our services. We had not been paid since I enlisted.. I guess the General felt we would enter combat soon and may need some money. The boats could take the money back to our families in Illinois and Ohio. I heard one of the Ohio sergeants say when they were fighting in Mexico they were always paid in gold or silver. Paper money wasn't always accepted, but regardless of where you were, everyone was glad to get good old U.S. gold coins. I guess the paymaster intended on giving each man one Eagle and three one dollar gold pieces for each month. There was probably enough money in these cases for two months pay to all of Grant's Army of The Tennessee.

What was I to do now? I had the entire payroll for the boys up there at Pittsburg Landing fighting and dying for their country. I felt fortunate to have the wagon with me. The Rebs would have certainly captured it, and these gold coins would have purchased a lot of rifles and ammunition from Canada and England that the Rebs would use to kill more Yankee boys. I sat and pondered my predicament. I had no rifle and no way of protecting the gold. The only thing I knew to do would be to hide the gold somewhere so the Rebs wouldn't find it.

As I slid off the box to the bottom of the wagon my hand touched a cloth bag. In it was the wagon crew's ration of biscuits, beans and salt pork. I was thankful for my good fortune and sat back and looked at the peaceful river while I thought of my next move. As I ate one of the biscuits and a piece of salt pork, it was difficult to think as the noise of battle to the north had not abated.

Chapter 4

I looked at the sun and figured it must be about 1:00. The battle was still raging, and I could only hope our boys were at least holding their own. I took a short walk on the rocky bank of the river. Just to my right I spotted a ledge under an over hang of stone. A tree had fallen and the limbs were hiding a flat surface of solid rock.. I knew if I was careful I could put all the money trunks on this ledge and cover them with tree limbs. It took quite an effort, but in about thirty minutes I had all the boxes shoved back completely out of sight. I raised the lids on the two opened boxes and took out five of the Gold Eagles and ten of the one dollar pieces. I didn't know my course of action, but I knew the money would come in handy. I had never had more than fifty cents in my pockets at any one time and that was when I was picking up some things at the store for mammaw.

I had no idea what would occur in my life next but my mind was clear. I had no reason to go home since Charley was dead, and I knew I was finished with war. I had no desire to shoot at anyone, and I wasn't ready to end up like Charley and all those brave boys lying in their own blood up there at Pittsburg Landing. If I was branded a coward then so be it. I figure I wouldn't be missed. After the battle there would be a lot of boys they wouldn't find. It looked to me like the Rebs were more cut out for battle than we were, and I figure this war wouldn't last much longer. I feel Mr. Lincoln will tire of so many of his boys dying and call this thing off. Somehow we will get back to normal and I hoped it wouldn't be too long in coming. I thought of the boy from Mississippi I had met when I was in the tenth grade. I knew Mississippi wasn't too far from Tennessee so I thought I would head in that direction. I doubt I could ever find that same boy, but I didn't know where else to go. I had to find me some other clothes and more food. If someone saw me in these blue pants with the yellow stripe down the side I would be shot on sight.

I marked my spot well and tried to make a crude map of the place. At the first chance I had I would notify our people up north that the gold was safe and where it could be picked up. This had to be the first landing south of Pittsburg, so they should be able to find it. I wouldn't mention the $60 I took. I figure I was due that for my trouble in saving so much of Mr. Lincoln's Gold from falling into Rebel hands.

In a pouch under the seat of the wagon I found a map of the area around Corinth. It looks like the plan had been to distribute the pay to the boys after Corinth was taken. This would be the reason the pay wagon was with Grant's Corps. The money had probably been on one of the boats as we came down the river. After today's battle, I doubt we will have enough boys left to take Corinth any time in the near future. The map showed Pittsburg Landing and the road southwest toward Corinth. I felt Corinth wouldn't be hospitable to me regardless of who owned it, Yank or Reb.

There was a town on the map just east of Corinth that shouldn't be too far from my present position. My decision was to wait until dark, dispose of the wagon, let one of the horses go and take the other one with me. Some time tonight I hoped I could find Iuka, Mississippi.

GENERAL U.S. GRANT'S ARMY CORPS

PITTSBURG LANDING, TENNESSEE– APRIL 8, 1862

General Grant and his entire staff assembled in a make shift mess hall on the shores of the Tennessee overlooking Pittsburg Landing to assess the outcome of the two day battle that had just ended the evening before. After initial major thrusts by the Confederate forces under the command on General Albert Sydney Johnston on Sunday morning April 6th the union forces were driven almost to the edge of the river. Word came that some time during that attack General Johnston was mortally wounded and died. His replacement, General Beauregard, stopped the attack of the 6th and drew his men back to decide on which course he should take to complete the victory. During the night of the 6[th,] General Don Carlos Buell arrived with 20,000 fresh Union troops. At dawn, on the 7th, also reinforced by General Lew Wallace's division, General Grant ordered a full attack against the entire line of Rebel forces. The surprised and seriously outnumbered Confederates fought hard throughout the day and then were ordered by General Beauregard to retreat and give up the battle. The tired and shaken men retired to Corinth, 25 miles to the south.

Information to Grant and his staff reported that the first estimate showed alarming casualties with at least 13,000 Union soldiers killed and many more wounded. The staff agreed that the Corps was in no condition to follow the southerners at this time, and a decision was made to carry the remaining members of the Corps back north a short distance to heal and refit for further action against the enemy.

As the meeting closed a staff officer reported that a pay wagon containing over $500,000 in gold coins had been confiscated by the Confederates during the battle. It was assumed it was carried to Corinth with the retreating Rebel army.

Chapter 5

I took the harnesses off the two horses and made a makeshift bridle, so I could ride bareback on one of the animals. I chose the brown roan with the white streak on the nose because he was the gentler of the two animals. I released the other horse as I had no means of caring for him. I hoped he would make his way back to our lines and be picked up by friendly hands. I decided it would not be wise to carry the wagon with me. The Reb cannon bursts had caused considerable damage to the frame, and the wild ride I had forced upon the vehicle was of no help either.

The water appeared to be very deep a few feet from the shore of the Tennessee, and I urged the wagon toward the water by reattaching my one horse to the harness and having him back up, pushing the wagon into the water. Just as the wagon slid over the rock shelf, I jumped from the seat and cut the harness from the horse with the bayonet. As I suspected the wagon slid harmlessly into the water and disappeared . The weight of the wheels and banding were enough to make the entire wagon sink. It would be doubtful it would ever be seen again.

I started my journey south on foot, leading my horse as I went. We came to a flat field of grass and the horse grazed for a while. It had probably been some time since he had eaten. I decided that at first chance I would secure him some proper food. He was a spirited animal yet very docile to the touch. We seemed to form an instant bond, and I decided to call him Charley in honor of my fallen friend.

As darkness approached I had no idea if I were still in Tennessee or had crossed into Mississippi. The map I took from the buckboard was crude and mostly covered the area immediately adjacent to Corinth. I still felt I was moving in the general direction of Iuka, but it was difficult to tell. Sometime around dusk I moved away from the sounds of the battle at Pittsburg Landing, so I knew I had traveled some distance. I tired slightly and slid on Charley`s back to ride a spell. Charley accepted me cordially and made no movement to dislodge me. I had ridden bareback quite a bit on the farm. We only owned one saddle and my daddy never let me use it. Charley's back was quite wide and made for a comfortable ride.

Some time during the night I spotted a light in a small farm house. The moon was very bright and the house and it's adjacent barn was easily visible to the eye. I quietly slid from the horse's back and looked in the barn, hoping to find some provisions. It was quite dark, but the moon coming from the south east offered enough light for me to see what was inside. Two horses stirred slightly in their stalls but made no noticeable noise that would give my presence away. Three saddles were hanging on spikes outside the stalls and a pair of overalls were draped beneath the bottom saddle. The overalls were about my size, so I eased them from the hook and also took what looked like the oldest of the saddles. I was certainly no thief and didn't want to deprive the owner of anything that would cause him distress. I found a piece of charcoal on the floor and wrote a crude note on a board.

"I hope you will accept this $10 as payment for the saddle and overalls. I am a traveler in need. Thank you."

I knew the $10 in gold was more than enough to cover the cost of the old saddle and the worn clothing. I could only hope the owner would not feel badly toward me.

I was quite tired from my ordeal of the day and felt the need for sleep. I tied the horse to a tree and lay down in soft grass. I folded the overalls and made a comfortable pillow. I readily fell into a deep sleep. A need to clear my bladder waked me at dawn, and I felt refreshed from the sound sleep. I decided to take up my journey again and started south past the house where I got the saddle and overalls.

By full daylight, I could see a small village nestled in a clump of trees with one road going north and south and one east and west. I had to assume this was Iuka in Mississippi. I took off my blue army pants and put the overalls over my long johns . I buried the pants and my cap under an oak tree and hoped I could pass as a regular traveler. I needed food and other clothes, and I had the money to buy them. I just hoped my speech and demeanor didn't give me away as an enemy. I felt no animosity toward these people, and it would be my hope they would feel the same toward me. Having been reared on a rural farm in Illinois I had grown to speak not a lot different from the southerners I had talked to at Fort Donelson. I felt with a little effort I could give the appearance of a bonafide Reb.

As I stood on the hill and looked at the town, I realized I was embarking on a new life. I would have to lie and pretend to be someone other than Marcus Wade from Galena, Illinois. Any deviation from this plan would cause me to be imprisoned or even killed as a deserter or spy. I had made my choice and was willing to do whatever necessary to start a new life for myself. As I approached the town I had a good feeling that some way I could pull this off.

There was a small square in the center of the town with a saloon, a dentist office, a harness and saddle store and what I was looking for, Swanson`s Mercantile. As I entered the store I realized it was sparsely stocked but adequate for my needs. I picked up two shirts, two pair of trousers, some socks, a new pair of long johns and a belt. I tried on a brimmed hat but thought better of it and left it on the shelf. As I moved toward the food section a pretty dark haired girl about my age spoke to me.

"Can I help you, young man? Looks like you need quite a lot there."

"Yessum," I replied in my best southern drawl. "I left all my things back home in Alabama when I left. Momma didn`t want me to go and daddy was mad at me. I didn`t get to bring anything with me."

I had rehearsed this speech in my mind all morning, and the young lady seemed to accept it.

"What happened that made you leave your home? You going to join up to fight the Yankee`s?"

"No, ma`am," I replied. "That`s what got me in trouble with paw. I ain`t got the heart for killin` and paw called me a coward. I had enough money saved up to pay off my conscription debt and I don`t have to join up if I don`t want to."

The young girl looked straight in my eyes, came around the counter and extended her hand. "Well, let me shake the hand of a sensible man," said the girl. "All the boys around here up and left as soon as the war broke out. Ain`t nobody left in town but some children and old coots too old to carry a gun. Where are you headed and what are you going to do?"

I ain't quite sure," I answered, realizing I had sold my story. I decided to see how far I could take it. "You don't know of any work around here do you? I would like to settle down and plant some roots somewhere. I can do just about anything on a farm."

The girl told me her name was Jenny Swanson. Jenny and her momma were trying to keep the store going while living on a thirty acre farm east of town. Jenny's daddy was killed by a horse kick to the head a few years ago, and her two brothers left home to join Bedford Forrest' regiment in Memphis. She said she would have to talk to her momma, but they sure could use some help out at the home place. She couldn't pay much but could provide good food and shelter, if I was interested. I told her I would really appreciate it, and the money wasn't any problem. I just needed a place to stay and something to do. She asked me my name and I told her Marcus Wade. I didn't see any need in changing my name way down here where nobody knew me anyway.

"Hi, Marcus," Jenny said. "Can you stay here a minute and watch the store while I run over to the saloon and talk to momma? She's over there at a meeting of the town ladies making bandages. Word just came in that there was a big skirmish up north on the river, and a lot of our boys were killed and wounded."

Jenny said a rider came by this morning and told the ladies he would be back tomorrow to pick things up and take the bandages to Corinth.

Her message kinda staggered me for a minute. I had tried to put the battle out of my mind, but I knew that would be impossible.

"Who won the battle?" I asked, feeling that after what I had seen by Shiloh Church there seemed little doubt the Rebs had driven Grant and his entire Corps into he river.

"I'm afraid the Yankees did," said Jenny. "The rider said there were hundreds killed and wounded and our boys had retreated and gone back to Corinth."

I tried to act calm, but the news unnerved me no end. For the first time since I jumped on that wagon and ran away from the battle, I felt like a coward. I didn't see any way our boys could hold back those charging, yelling men in gray. I felt there was no way we could have won the battle at Pittsburg Landing.

I turned to the side, so Jenny couldn`t see my reaction to her news of the battle. I reached on a shelf for a can of peaches.

"Sure, Jenny, you go on and talk to your momma. I`ll watch the store for you," I said, still shaken by the news of the battle.

Jenny slipped out the door and quickly headed toward the saloon. I put the can of peaches on the counter and tried to gather my wits.

Should I go back to the battlefield and rejoin my unit? What about the gold? Will they believe I didn`t try to steal it? How can I explain leaving my unit and running away? What would Lieutenant Ames say when I tell him I can`t shoot anyone?

I knew my story would be hard to accept. I had heard the Ohio boys say that a deserter would be shot by a firing squad at dawn. Would my own countrymen really shoot me just because I didn`t have the heart for war?

I spotted Jenny leaving the saloon with an older lady at her side. I figured it must be her momma. I knew if I could find refuge here in this remote part of the country, I had better accept it. Somehow, I could lose myself in this place and make some kind of sense of my life. I knew now I could never return to Illinois. Whatever future I had would be as a southerner.

Jenny and the older lady came in the store, and you could see Jenny had taken a lot of her good looks from her momma. Mrs. Swanson was a little taller than Jenny, but any one could tell they were kin folk. Jenny`s mom spoke first.

"Hi, Marcus. Jenny tells me you have the need of a place to lay your head. Are you a good boy who knows how to work?"

"Yes ma`am, Mrs. Swanson. I have worked all my life and wouldn`t expect to stop now. You don`t have to worry about me. I have no taste for strong drink, and I will do my best to help you and your daughter find life more hospitable."

"Why, young man, what a nice way you have with words. Come sit with me over some coffee, and let us discuss your future."

Jenny was grinning as she went behind the counter and handed us two cups of coffee. Mrs. Swanson and I sat at a small table that was evidently used by customers to sit and pass the day. I found that Mrs. Swanson`s name was Agnes, and she and Jenny had tried to maintain the store and small farm since her boys left to fight with General Forrest. She told me she thought about selling the farm, but it had been in her family for years, and she had no heart for disposing of it. The store was her husbands before they married and since his untimely death, she and Jenny had tried to keep it open. Business had always been good before the war, but now there weren't that many people who had any money to spend on dry goods. When the war started in '61, the State of Mississippi had issued it's own money and most of her trade was in the these new Confederate dollars. Mrs. Swanson said things were going well until some of the drummers who brought her merchandise insisted they be paid in gold or silver. She rarely received gold and silver anymore so her status as a business lady was on shaky ground.

I thought of Mr. Lincoln's Gold up on the river bank and wished I had brought more of it to give to this good woman.

We agreed I would live at the farm and raise corn and tend the garden. I would keep the place clean and in good order. In exchange, I would eat the same food as Jenny and Mrs. Swanson and live in the back room where the two brothers had lived. The Swanson's had two milk cows and one mule. I told Mrs. Swanson about my horse, Charley, and she was pleased I could use Charley for plowing and transportation. Mrs. Swanson said she would try to pay me $5 a month if she had enough left after her expenses at the store.

When Jenny totaled my bill for the clothes and peaches it came to $4.25. I thought it best not to pull out a ten dollar gold piece, so I gave her five of the one dollar coins. Mrs. Swanson's eyes brightened when she saw the shiny coins.

"I haven't seen real gold money in six months. Where did you get this, son?"

I knew I had to continue my lie, and I had already prepared a story for this question.

"I raised some good horses back home, and I sold them for enough gold to pay my $100 conscription fee and have fifty dollars left over. I figure I still got close to $40 of it left," I said. "You are welcome to it, if you need the money, Mrs. Swanson."

I could tell Mrs. Swanson was touched by my offer, but I had given it in good faith. I had no need for funds and these good people had offered me a roof over my head and food to eat.

I think I saw a tear in the corner of Jenny's eye when she handed me my package of clothes. We talked of the directions out to the farm and I felt I would have no trouble finding the place. As I was walking out the door, I stepped on a pecan that had fallen from a basket. I looked down and froze in my tracks. I looked at my shoes. They were U.S. Government issue. Any sharp eye could tell what they were and where they had come from.

Chapter 6

Mrs. Swanson noticed the expression on my face and asked me if something was wrong. I tried ro recover my wits and told her the inside of my shoes had been rubbing my feet and when I stepped on the pecan it just hurt a bit.

"What size shoe do you wear?" asked Mrs. Swanson.

I told her I wore a 9 but could get by with a 10. Mrs. Swanson walked over to a rack of shoes and pulled a brown pair of good quality work shoes from the shelf and handed them to me.

"These should do nicely," she said. "We wouldn't want our new farm hand to have sore feet all the time."

I thanked Mrs. Swanson, took the shoes, and hurried out the door. I didn't want Jenny and her mother to look at my old shoes any more. I realized how lucky I was that my lie hadn't been discovered. I got on Charley and headed east in the direction of the farm. Jenny's directions were easily followed, and I had little problem finding the Swanson place.

The farm was relatively small with a substantial house and barn and a few acres of plowed ground inside a clump of trees. It wasn't any bigger than grandpa's place back in Galena but was much prettier and certainly better kept. Someone had made sure there was no trash laying around and the porch of the house had been recently swept. I put my package of clothes on a chair on the porch and went in the unlocked front door of the house. I wasn't surprised to see a spotless room with a nice sofa and two chairs. The spacious fireplace was made with beautiful odd shaped stones. I had noticed these same stones in the hillsides on my sojourn from Pittsburg Landing. There were two matching oil lamps on tables by the chairs. There was another lamp on the mantle over the fireplace. The kitchen was to the right of the fireplace. There was a heavy iron stove and a sink with a pump mounted on the side. I pushed up and down on the pump and clean water flowed from the spout. We never had water running into our house back in Illinois. I figured Mr. Swanson or his boys had worked out a system where they attached on to the well some way so water was available to the pump.

23

I recognized a cabinet like Charley Rogers' folks had back in Galena. It was white metal with doors on the bottom that had pans and bowls stacked inside. A large flat shelf served as a work counter. I pulled the shelf and it slid out making a larger surface. The top also had doors with shelves inside. Jenny and Mrs. Swanson had neatly stacked glasses, plates and cups and saucers in the left side and the right cabinet had flour, sugar, salt, pepper and other things used in cooking. In the center opening of the top cabinet was a flour sifter with a handle. I remembered how Charley and me had made such a mess at his house one day playing with the sifter. I looked at the metal plate on the top rim of the cabinet, and it had the familiar words "Hoosier Cabinet" stamped in it. I never did know what that meant, but the cabinet was some kind of wonderful contraption.

The table was made of four eight inch poplar boards about six feet long. Good sturdy poplar legs supported the table. There were four matching poplar chairs around the table and one more just like them pulled over against the wall by the Hoosier Cabinet. I figured the five chairs had been for Jenny and her mother and the two brothers who had gone to fight with General Forrest and their daddy who was kicked in the head by the horse.

At the north end of the room was a short hall leading to two bedrooms and a small wash room. There was also a pump handle over a large zinc tub and an iron wood stove in the corner where the water could be heated for a bath. There was even a smaller sink with a mirror over it for face washing and things. I pulled the curtain back in the wash room window and saw the privy right outside the window. It was real handy to the house with the back door not thirty feet from the outhouse. At our old house in Galena our privy was out by the chicken house. On cold mornings my feet would almost freeze as I made a much needed dash to the little outhouse. We never had any kind of wash room in our house or grandpa's house. We had a large zinc tub much like the one here. It was usually left just outside the back door and once a week we would pour cold water in the tub and quickly scrub off. In the cold winter, when he wasn't drunk, daddy would put the tub inside the back door. I can truthfully say I never saw my daddy willfully get in that tub. Sometimes when he was drunk, momma and me would strip him and roll him over into the tub and scrub him all over with lye soap.

The two bedrooms here at Jenny's house were just alike with two beds in each. I tried to figure where Jenny had slept when her two brothers and daddy were there. I knew Mr. and Mrs. Swanson would be in one of the rooms and the two brothers in the other. Maybe Jenny slept on the sofa in front of the fireplace.

It was easy to determine which room had been for the boys. There were still some of their clothes in the closet and a few things laying around that could only belong to boys. The bedrooms were a bit close to each other for my comfort. I had looked at Jenny's ample figure under her gingham dress. I had no mind to cause distress around the home by me seeing her or her seeing me coming naked out of the washroom. Except for the skinny dipping we did with Charley and his sister, Maggie, down in the creek, I had no experience with an unclothed female near my age. We had been doing this since we were six or seven. None of us really ever noticed there was a difference in the way we were put together. I had no time to spark the girls in Galena.

It surprised me when I had that tingling feeling in my stomach when I looked at Jenny. I had no explanation for it but I knew these people were providing me a new life for myself, and I didn't need to be gawking at Jenny and her mother with any lusting in my mind. I remember how Preacher Renshaw would talk on the subject of lusting, and I finally figured out what he meant one day when Charley said he had a craving to crawl into the hay loft with May Beth Jackson and see what was under all those clothes. I doubt Charley ever saw more than a bunch of thick petticoats, since he didn't say more on the subject.

I walked out the back door and strolled the short distance to the barn. The two huge doors leading to the stalls were open, and I could see the two cows and mule grazing in the field just behind the barn. Jenny or her mother must come out in the mornings, milk the cows and let them loose in the field for the day. Hay bales were stacked against the front of the stalls for the cows to munch on and provide food during bad weather. I wondered where the hay had come from. I couldn't see enough land around to provide for feed grass. All the exposed land I saw had been cultivated for food or money crops. The small grazing field behind the barn certainly wouldn't produce hay like this. I assumed some kind neighbor had brought the hay bales to Mrs. Swanson.

The tack room was right inside the entrance to the barn. It was very orderly with harnesses, cruppers and bits hanging from large spikes driven in the heavy walls. A long flat blanket chest was built in under the one window, and I knew the top of this would do nicely for my bed. The room was clean, tight against the elements, and had a nice homey smell to it. The lantern hanging on the support post was full of oil. I knew this would be my abode for whatever time I was allowed to stay here. I had crossed a serious line today. Somehow, I had to convince one and all I was Marcus Wade from Alabama, and not a deserter from Mr. Lincoln's Union Army.

Chapter 7

By the time Jenny and her mother arrived home I had taken a mattress off one of the boy's beds and placed it on the top of the blanket chest. I found adequate bedding to make for a comfortable sleep. This accommodation would feel quite nice compared to the months of sleeping on the ground in Mr. Lincoln's army. There was a spirited discussion between myself and Jenny about me not sleeping in the comfort of her brother's bedroom, but Mrs. Swanson made little contribution to the argument. I feel Mrs. Swanson could see the problems ahead if Jenny and I were confided in too close surroundings. The decision was made that I would sleep in the barn but would eat all my meals with the ladies. Arrangements would be made for me to use the washroom on Saturday evenings while the ladies were tending to their darning and reading in the front of the house. I made a little sign to go on the door of the privy with an arrow that pointed to the word 'occupied'. There was also a substantial wooden turn knob on the inside that the occupant of the privy could turn and adequately lock the door.

With all the living arrangements decided upon, I threw myself into the task of becoming the man of the house for Jenny Swanson and her mother. Early April was a good time for me to arrive as I was able to use the plow to prepare the land for the corn crop. My horse, Charley, accepted the harness without rebuke and proved to be a better than adequate plow horse. He seemed to enjoy getting out each morning and leading the plow. He was powerful and yet gentle. He had taken a liking to Jenny and was always happy to see her arrive with his treat of a fresh apple each day. There were adequate oats in the barn for Charley, and he was actually living a much better life than when he worked as a Union Army horse.

Charley also liked the days when we hooked up the family buckboard and made weekly trips into Iuka for supplies. On one such trip I thought my past had been discovered when Mr. Adams, at the Harness Shop, came out and admired Charley.

"Why, this is one fine animal," said Mr. Adams. "You don't see prime stock like this around these days. They have all been confiscated for the army."

I explained to Mr. Adams that this was my own horse I had raised in Alabama. I thought this would suffice until Mr. Adams said he had grown up on a farm in north Alabama and asked me what town I had come from. I can truthfully say I knew nothing about the state of Alabama and certainly didn't know the names of any towns. The Lord was with me as my mind switched to a box in the tack room where a trace chain was stored. The box had the name of some company in Birmingham, Alabama.

"We lived on a farm outside Birmingham," I said sheepishly to Mr. Adams. I couldn't tell by the expression on his face whether he believed me or not. Evidently he did. Mr. Adams continued to admire Charley and never mentioned my former abode again. I felt I had passed a serious test that day.

Jake, the mule, was helpful for light weight work. He didn't have the power Charley had but had been raised with the plow and quickly answered my commands. It was surprising how the terms Gee and Haw meant the same thing to a southern mule as it did to one in Illinois. The amazing thing about Jake was how friendly he was. The mule we had in Galena was ornery and cantankerous and didn't like people around. He did his work and then wanted to be left alone. Jake liked people and every time Jenny or I would walk out to the barn Jake would sidle up to us for a pat on the head. Jake would see Jenny give Charley an apple and nudge her under the arm until she relented and gave him one, too. It became a daily game for Jenny and me, and we enjoyed our time with our four legged friends.

Jenny had two dogs she said just showed up about three years ago. They were almost identical little brown terrier type dogs that were obviously brother and sister. They loved the farm and spent most of their time running from field to field yapping at each other as they went. They took to me immediately and both slept by my bed in the tack room. My daddy had never let me have a dog of my own and I was loving having these two friends who never saw anything but the best side of everything. They were eternally happy and looked forward to every day of life. Occasionally we fed the dogs table scraps but they were quite good at catching varmints in and around the barn.

Will, the oldest of Jenny's brothers, must have been about my size as his clothes fit me just right. Agnes insisted I wear his things as he was well equipped with a rain slicker, a light denim jacket and a heavy coat for winter. He also had a pair of rubber boots that were handy around the barn. At first, I was reluctant to wear another man's clothes but soon it became the quite normal thing to do.

Word came in early June that Corinth had fallen to the Yankees. The battle had raged since late April and Beauregard finally realized he had no other course but to surrender the garrison to the Federal troops. Mr. Adams at the Harness shop said this was a tragic day for the Confederacy. The railroad junction was vital to the Rebel forces, and with it's loss, it would be virtually impossible to transport much needed supplies to the soldiers in the field. The people in Iuka said they were afraid Iuka would see Union soldiers looking for supplies. Many of the residents buried their valuables and hid extra food stuffs in the thick woods around the town.

The corn crop was quite bountiful. Rain came at the right time and the seed the Swanson boys kept from earlier crops was of top grade. We had early food corn for the table and Jenny and I would sit on the porch scraping corn from the ears into the big wash pan for Mrs. Swanson to cook up and put away in jars for the winter. I had always liked corn. The way Mrs. Swanson prepared it with flour, salt, pepper and a little sugar was certainly wonderful to the taste. We enjoyed fresh corn on the cob and with our ample garden of vegetables we ate quite well. Mrs. Swanson would swap corn and other vegetables with the Shepherd family about a mile down the road for ham and sausage and an occasional strip of tenderloin. Mr. Shepherd had a hog farm and provided a lot of the meat for the people in the area. Jenny or her mother would cook an occasional fresh pie or cake and wonderful flat sugar cookies. I liked the cornbread my Mammaw cooked back home, but it didn't compare to Mrs. Swanson's. I don't know what she put in it, but with the homemade butter Jenny churned, it was tasty indeed.

Life on the farm was true heaven for me. I was doing what I knew how to do and the war was far away. Mrs. Swanson's business was suffering, but our life on the farm was comfortable, happy and peaceful. Jenny and I had become quite close and it was evident we had were now more than just friends. One night in early September we were out by the barn and Jenny spoke the first words about our relationship.

"Do you have a girl friend back in Alabama, Marcus?" Jenny asked.

"No, Jenny. I have never had a girl friend before you."

"Am I your girlfriend, Marcus? Do you really care for me as I care for you?"

I knew then we had crossed the line and would never turn back. Somehow I had to tell Jenny who I really was and keep no secrets from her, but I knew that now was not that time. I pulled Jenny close, and we kissed for the first time. I had never kissed a girl before, and yet, what we did was as natural as breathing. A feeling rushed over me that totally consumed me. I had heard people speak of love. I didn't know what it was, but I knew this girl in my arms was now my life and I would do anything in my power to protect her and make her happy. In the eyes of the world I was a coward. I lied about my past and I guess I was a thief. I had taken $60 of Mr. Lincoln's Gold and hadn't told anyone where the rest of the money was. I had no remorse about my former life. I felt I was an American but I was also an American living here in Mississippi. Why did we have to be at war? Why couldn't I tell Jenny about my former life and move on to our own happiness? Would she hate me if she knew I were a former enemy soldier? I knew some day I would have to answer all these questions, but I also knew I couldn't risk losing Jenny now. For the first time in my life, another human being truly loved me. I wasn't going to let that love get away for any reason. Right now, I simply couldn't tell Jenny who I really was.

"Oh, Jenny, I love you so. I have loved you since the first day I saw you in the store. I know you must love me, too."

"I do, Marcus. I do love you. The last five months have been the happiest days of my life. You have made my life complete, and I never want to be away from you."

Jenny poured out her heart to me. We both knew at that moment regardless of any of the problems facing us we had to be together forever.

"I want to tell mother how we feel, Marcus. She will know things between us can never be the way it was."

Mrs. Swanson was sitting on the porch on this pretty warm September night when Jenny and I walked up the steps. Jenny didn't hesitate.

"Momma. Marcus and I are in love. I truly love him, and he loves me. Is it all right with you?"

In the months I had known Agnes Swanson, I gained a tremendous respect for her. She was a hard working business lady, a good mother to Jenny, and a fair and helpful friend to me. I wasn't surprised by her answer.

"Well, bless your hearts. I have been watching you for these past months, and I knew it was just a matter of time until you two realized what had developed between you was true love. Of course, it is all right with me. I, too, love Marcus and would be pleased to have him as my son- in- law."

Jenny cried and raced to her mother and engulfed her in her arms. They laughed and hugged tightly and reached out to draw me into the circle of love. On the porch of the Swanson home in rural North East Mississippi, I knew my life would never be the same after this night. I was going to have to solve many personal problems and try to bury many ghosts of the past, but somehow I had to do it. Jenny was now too precious to me. Whatever it took I knew I couldn't let her go.

On that special night we couldn't imagine the hardships that would befall us in coming days.

The Confederate soldiers started arriving in Iuka on September the 14th. We heard that General Sterling Price's Army of the West had been ordered by his superior, General Braxton Bragg, to set up a defensive position in Iuka to halt the advance of Union General William Rosecrans. Rosecrans was on his way to join Buell's Army of the Ohio. Bragg was determined to rout Buell and his garrison in Nashville and didn't want Buell to receive the extra manpower from Rosecrans. General Grant learned of Bragg's intentions from a spy traveling with Price`s Army of the West and devised a plan of his own to attack Price in northeastern Mississippi.

On September 19 a bitter battle broke out between Confederate General Price and Union General Rosecrans` armies with heavy casualties on both sides. With the news of the Union reinforcements arrival, Price had his men depart the area during the night and advance to Ripley to join with Maj. General Van Dorn`s Corps to fight another day when the odds were better in his favor.

After the battle Rosecrans` Army occupied Iuka for three days during which time they looted and plundered everything of value in the town. The shelves in Swanson`s Mercantile were left bare. The Union soldiers even took the dress fabric and ladies shoes. The shelves of canned foods and barrels of pickles, lard, flour and sugar were carried away by the Union soldiers.

The Yankees didn`t get out to the farm, so the home place was spared, but the future seemed bleak with the loss of the store`s merchandise.

Rosecran`s Army departed the ravished town on September 22nd in pursuit of the retreating Confederates.

On October 3rd combined Rebel forces including Van Dorn and Price attacked Corinth in an attempt to re-capture the vital rail center. In bitter fighting the Confederates were repulsed and Corinth remained in the hands of the Union forces.

Chapter 8

The news of the two boy's deaths came on October 9th. A rider came by the house with a casualty list and a note from General Forrest's aide expressing his sorrow in the loss of Will and Frank Swanson. They had both died in a Cavalry attack on Yankee positions in a remote outpost in Tennessee.

The news was particularly devastating to Agnes. She hadn't said much about the boys in the months I had been there, and only on two occasions had she received letters from them. It was as if she had expected this day to come. She thought she was prepared for it, but the actual news of it broke her heart. She closed herself in her room and didn't come out for three days. Jenny tried to take Agnes some food, but she wouldn't eat. Finally, on the fourth day she came in the kitchen, fixed a cup of coffee, and called Jenny and me to her at the kitchen table.

"I knew when my boys went off to fight in the war I would never see them again," Agnes said. "Now they are gone, and for what? What good did it do the great Confederate States of America for my two boys to charge into a Yankee bullet and give their lives in a lost cause. We can't win this war and our lives won't ever be the same again?"

Agnes paused, took another sip of coffee and a bite of bread and continued.

"You two young people must marry and enjoy what happiness you can here on the farm. There is no way we can re-stock the store and the bank will have to take the building over when I can't repay the loan payment in December."

Agnes paused, got up, and walked to the window and looked out. Then she said.

" The Yankees have taken everything from us, and all we have is what we can live on here on the farm. We still have the animals and a good seed stock for the crops. Somehow, we will make it."

I stood, walked over and put my arm around Agnes' shoulder and pulled her close. I knew the time had come for me to tell the truth about who I was.

"Agnes, I want you and Jenny to sit with me and let me tell you my real life's story."

Jenny looked up at me as if she had just seen me for the first time. Agnes moved to the sofa and pulled Jenny down on the seat beside her. She too had a puzzled look on her face. I sat in the chair facing them. I wasn't afraid now to tell the truth about my life. I knew I could make a tremendous difference in the lives of these people I loved with all my heart, and somehow I had to hope they would accept me for who I really was. I spoke without hesitation.

"When I walked into your store that day back in April, I was a desperate man. I only entered your store because I had to have clothes and supplies. I never dreamed you would offer me a job and a place to stay. I did not intend to deceive you, but if I had told you the truth about who I really was, I know I would not be here now. I can only hope when you hear my story you will forgive my lies and let me stay and love you both forever."

Jenny and Agnes sat stunned. They didn't say anything but stared directly into my eyes. I continued.

"The only true thing I told you that day was my name. I am Marcus Wade, but I have never been to Alabama. I was born in a small town in Illinois named Galena. I was raised on a farm and because of my drunken daddy, and his cruelty to me, I was forced to live with my grandparents until I got out of high school. I hated my life there and only had one true friend, a very special boy named Charley Rogers."

I told Agnes and Jenny my entire story from the time I entered the army until that day at Pittsburg Landing when I witnessed the horror of the battle and how I saw Charley killed by the cannon blast. I related how I got in the wagon and sped away to save my hide. I told them I had never really wanted to join the army, and I knew I could never shoot and kill another human being. I spoke about how I decided that I was through with war. I then told of finding Mr. Lincoln's Gold in the back of the wagon.

"Why, I was dumbstruck when I saw all that money. I didn't mean to steal any of the Union's money, but it just happened that way. Nobody saw me in that buckboard, and I figure the Yanks think the Rebs got it. I'm sure it's still hid on the river bank right where I left it."

Jenny and Agnes still couldn't speak. I know they were mortified to think they had been living with a Yankee soldier all this time, but they were so stunned by my story they just sat there. I told the whole story of how I put sixty dollars in my pocket and how I still had forty of it in my poke out in the barn.

"If you will let me stay, I plan to go to the river and get enough of Mr. Lincoln's Gold to re-stock the store and let you fix things up a little. I know now I can never tell the Union authorities about the gold. It is too late for that. I would just get myself shot as a spy."

I got up and walked to the door. I had told the story as truthfully as I could, and I knew if Agnes and Jenny wanted to, they could stop the next Reb soldier that came by and have me arrested. I really didn't know what to expect. Jenny was the first to get up and walk toward me. I thought she might slap me across the face, but she put her arms around me and pulled me close.

"Oh, Marcus, my love. What a heavy burden you have had to carry all this time. I don't care where you came from. I know you love me and will protect me forever. I still love you and want to be your wife."

Agnes also came over to me. She pulled me close and stroked my hair. I knew she had accepted my story and forgave me for my lies. For the first time in my life I felt I had a real family.

We sat and talked a while longer, and when Agnes went to bed, I turned to Jenny and said,

"Will you marry me right away, Jenny? I promise I will never lie to you again. I won't promise you I will take up arms against the Union, but I will protect you and Agnes, no matter what."

"Yes, I'll marry you, Marcus. Yes, yes, yes!"

I went to bed that night feeling better than I had felt in months. The lies of my past had finally come out, and Jenny and Agnes stilled loved me. I knew at that moment I would make a difference in the lives of these people I loved so dearly.

Chapter 9

Jenny and I were married on October the 16th, 1862, in the little Baptist church in Iuka. There were just a few people present, but it was a happy affair. Jenny and Agnes and I decided not to tell the other people in Iuka about my past. Maybe later, but not now. On our wedding night, Agnes stayed in town with Mrs. Adams in their spare room behind the harness shop.

Jenny and I shared our love for each other as naturally as if we had been lovers for years. We knew we had done the right thing by marrying. I could now be the true man of the house and take care of Jenny and Agnes. If the war had not been going on it would have been heaven on earth. Jenny and I moved into her brother's old room.

Jenny said it was too dangerous for me to go and try to get the gold, but I knew the route to the river was free of soldiers from both sides. After the second battle of Corinth, there was no military action in the area. There was no reason for anyone to suspect I was doing anything but making a normal ride to pick up supplies. We loaded the buckboard with a few sandwiches and some water. I hooked Charley to the wagon and struck out on the morning of the 20th of October. There was a chill in the air, but all in all it was a nice ride. I had no trouble finding the small road to the river and in less than six hours from the time I left Iuka, I was pulling the brush back from the rock shelf and looking directly at the trunks holding Mr. Lincoln's Gold. I decided to get one trunk each of the ten dollar Eagles and the dollar coins. It would be easier to explain the smaller coins to most people.

For some reason, the trunks didn't seem as heavy as they were when I had unloaded them. I guess I was in a little better shape now than the day of the great battle. I put the two trunks in the back of the wagon and put the brush covering back over the makeshift cave in the river wall. I stood on the rock ledge and peered into the river where I had pushed the wagon. There was no evidence that a wagon had ever been there. I knew then the wagon would never be discovered. I urged Charley forward and started my journey back to Iuka.

I met with no difficulty and arrived back home a little before midnight. Agnes and Jenny usually retired around nine each night, but they were both waiting for me out by the barn when Charley pulled the wagon inside. Jenny kissed me and Agnes put her arm on my shoulder.

"Did you have any trouble, son?" Agnes asked.

I don't know why, but when I heard her call me son, it was difficult for me to hold back the tears. I think my real mother loved me in some way, but I knew now this lovely southern lady truly loved me. I vowed in my heart I would never betray that love. I answered without her knowing how deeply I had been touched.

"None at all. All the money was right where I left it. Come here, I want you to see what $75,000 in gold looks like."

I opened the two trunks and handed Jenny a box of the Eagles and Agnes a box of the one dollar pieces. They both stood spellbound. I imagine $500 was the most either of them had ever seen at one time, and the sight of the beautiful gold coins was quite a shock.

"My, my," said Agnes. "They are quite pretty, aren't they?"

We talked for a few minutes about what we would do with all the coins, and it was decided we better destroy the government boxes and bury the coins out by the tree line. I took some old burlap bags that seed came in and put the small, unmarked boxes of coins in them. It was late, but we all thought we would feel better if we got our job done this night. I had Charley pull the wagon across the grazing field to the trees. It only took about twenty minutes to bury the sacks of coins. They would be easy to recover when we needed them. I chopped up the Government trunks with the axe and burned them on the trash pile. When I was sure there was no evidence of any U.S. Government marks, I unhooked Charley from the wagon, washed off at the pump, and went inside where Jenny had cooked me three eggs and some bacon. I ate it all before Jenny and I retired to our room for the night. It had been quite a day.

Agnes explained what we would have to do to re-stock the store. The drummer's selling goods would be passing by soon, and she would have to order the needed things at that time. The merchandise would have to be brought in on a large wagon as the quantity would be more than a drummer could carry in his small rig. It was decided we wouldn`t order everything at once. An initial payout of $600 in gold would not raise too many eyebrows. Agnes could say she had been saving through the years for just such an emergency. The bank note of $300 would be paid later in December, so people wouldn`t talk about all the good fortune that had befallen widow Swanson. By doling out the money in small amounts, we figured we would not arouse anyone`s suspicions.

Jenny and I knew there was more money buried out by the fence than we could probably spend in a lifetime. After much talk and discussion with Agnes, we decided when we could we would try to help some families who had been hurt the most by the war. We didn`t know exactly how we would do it, but on that night we started making plans.

The first salesman came by on October 25th. The weather had taken a change for the worse and a cold north wind was blowing across the porch of the store. I had gone to the store with Agnes and Jenny, so I could help with the decision making about re-stocking. The drummer worked for a company out of Birmingham that sold almost anything a small store could use. He lived at Florence and traveled all across north Alabama and Mississippi. He told Agnes the war had made goods hard to get, and the prices would be somewhat higher than what she had paid in the past. He also said his boss, Mr. Ritter, said to get gold, silver or U.S. Dollars for the merchandise. He wasn`t allowed to accept Confederate money anymore.

Agnes and I talked of this earlier and thought that might be the case. We knew this arrangement would be of benefit to us.

Agnes ordered a basic stock of clothes, piece goods, hats, shoes and sundries such as buttons and zippers. The warehouse in Birmingham also carried a full line of canned goods and barrels of pickles, flour, apples and sugar. After the drummer totaled up the order, the bill came to a little over $700. As was the wholesaler`s custom, Agnes paid the drummer half of the money the day the order was placed and paid the balance when the shipment came on November the 10th. The drummer made no comment about all the shiny gold pieces. He simply accepted them and thanked Agnes for the business. He expressed his sorrow at the loss of the former merchandise to the Yankee`s and said he hoped he and his company could remain her primary supplier in the future.  The salesman also offered his condolences at the loss of the Agnes` two sons I couldn`t quite figure this fellow out. He appeared to be about thirty five years old and in perfect health. I wonder how he had been able to avoid service in the Rebel army. I assumed he had paid the $100 conscription fee.

There wasn`t a lot going on at the farm in November. We laid back the corn and hay and pretty much had things under control. I stayed in town most every day helping Jenny and Agnes unpack, price, and put the merchandise on the shelves. I had never had a lot of nice things in my life and to see this much at one time caused quite a stir in my stomach.   A lot of the town folk came in to see the new things, and by the end of the first week Agnes said she had sold almost $400 in merchandise. She felt that was a good start.

Agnes gladly took the Confederate money most of the customers used. Although we hadn`t touched any more of Mr. Lincoln`s Gold, we knew it was there, and it eased the thought that if the Confederate money proved worthless we could just let Mr. Lincoln make it up.

Chapter 10

Although war was raging throughout the country, you would never know it in Iuka, Mississippi. There were no troops in the area and only when an occasional rider came into town with bad news was there any indication our nation was still at war.

It was the week before Christmas and Jenny said she wanted an old fashion Christmas tree for our first Christmas together. We hooked Charley up to the wagon and made our way to the large cedar thicket south east of town. Jenny picked out the tree she wanted, and I got the axe and spade from the wagon and started felling the tree. Jenny wandered a short distance away and I heard her scream so loud I am sure they heard her in town. I ran to her side and immediately found what had caused her distress. There at the base of a large cedar was the body of a Yankee soldier curled up as if he were asleep. Sitting against the tree was another body. I thought it was probably the young man's comrade, but on closer inspection I could see the CSA on the man's cap. Both bodies were pretty gruesome to the eye with just a little flesh left covering the bones. The boys had evidently been killed in the Battle of Iuka in September. We had experienced very little rain since that time, so the uniforms were in reasonably good stead.

The Yank's uniform was much like the one I had been issued back in Illinois. I found no markings on his sleeve to tell his regiment, but the crossed swords on his hat indicated he was infantry. I looked carefully throughout his uniform and found nothing giving his name or where he was from. His Springfield rifle was by his side and his cartridge belt was full. If he had fired his gun at all, it wasn't evident. His blanket, back pack and grub sack were not to be found. It was my immediate opinion the boy had left his things on the battlefield and somehow made his way to this point. It is even possible the Reb could have shot him as he approached.

The Reb's outfit was far less like a uniform than his Yank opponent. The Rebs I had seen up at Fort Donelson had on neat all gray uniforms, but the boys I saw at Pittsburg Landing and the one dead here by the tree had very little that matched. The only thing gray the lad had on was the cap with CSA on it. The young man's shirt was what my Mammaw called homespun. It was well made and on the left pocket was the young man's name and unit:

> Jedediah Tomkins
> Company B
> First Alabama Infantry

Some loving hand had sewn this information on the boy's shirt. The Reb's blanket and grub sack were by his side. You could see where squirrels and other varmints had finished whatever food there was in the poke. The boy had the stub of a pencil hanging from his boney right hand and folded on his lap was a notebook. I picked up the notebook and opened it. The rain had smudged the writing a bit but the heavy cardboard cover had protected all of the inside pages. I recognized the book as one much like the one we used in school back in Illinois. My heart sank as I read the first line;

"To My Dearest Mother----

I closed the book quickly. I had no stomach to continue prying into this poor boy's affairs. He had obviously written his last letter to his mother.

Jenny saw my despair and walked to me. She could see the tear I couldn't keep from moving down my cheek.

"Marcus, what is wrong? What have you found?"

I handed Jenny the book without saying a word. She opened it and saw the writing on the first page. Jenny slowly closed the book and held it to her bosom.

"Oh, Marcus. This poor boy has written his mother, and she will never see it. Shall we bury it here with him?"

We discussed it briefly and decided we would bury the boys and carry the notebook back to the house and let Agnes decide what we should do. The weather had freshened and a cool breeze was coming from the north west. The ground was soft around the trees, and it took little effort to dig holes deep enough for the boy's remains. I buried the Yank's Springfield rifle by his side. I had Mr. Swanson's shotgun to use for hunting rabbits and squirrels, and I knew I could never use the Springfield to harm another person. After we covered them, Jenny said she would make some suitable crosses, and we could come back soon and place them over the boys. We could bring Agnes and let her say some words over them.

Jenny and I hardly spoke as we finished our grim task. We loaded our tree on the wagon and urged Charley on toward the farm. On the ride back to the farm Jenny sat holding the notebook to her chest. Many thoughts compassed our minds as we thought of the two young boys. Both the young men had been born in this country at about the same time, one in the north and one in the south. Because of this senseless war, they were now laying in a cedar thicket in a remote part of Mississippi where their bodies would never be seen again by family or friend.

SEPTEMBER 19, 1862— BATTLE OF IUKA, MISSISSIPPI
B COMPANY- FIRST ALABAMA INFANTRY

Jedediah Tomkins marched proudly with his company as they approached Iuka, Mississippi. Jedediah had joined Captain Marsh Stevens in A Company of the First Alabama Infantry four months prior. Captain Stevens said he was going to call Private Tomkins, Jed, since Jedediah sounded too much like a preacher and right now he needed fighting men more than preachers.

Jedediah enjoyed his stint in the Confederate Army. He met some fine men from all over northern Alabama, and he knew his regiment would hold themselves in good stead when called upon. First Alabama hadn`t been involved in battle as yet, but Captain Stevens said that was about to change. The Regiment had been ordered to join General Sterling Price at Iuka to stop Yankee General Rosecrans from advancing to Nashville. Spirits were high as the men approached the outskirts of the small town in the northeastern corner of Mississippi.

Jedediah thought it strange that he had been training and marching throughout central Alabama near Birmingham but was now within twenty miles of his home in Cherokee. He remembered as a boy hearing his daddy say he had to drive the rig over to Iuka, Mississippi to pick up a harness for the mule team. Jedediah realized the first Yankee he would see would be close to his home ground.

B Company moved to the right flank of the regiment. As they advanced into Iuka they were surprised by a line of blue clad soldiers suddenly appearing in the woods just north of their position. Captain Stevens was as shaken as the men in the ranks and made the only command he thought advisable. He ordered B Company to charge the Yankee position. It was a decision that would prove unwise and cause the loss of over eighty percent of the company. The Yankees had two batteries of cannon on the high ground and dispensed deadly fire on the charging Rebels.

Jedediah saw his sergeant blown in half by a cannon shell and the force of the blast threw Jedediah to the ground. When he arose, he ran to his right trying to gain some ground going up the hill. He looked west and realized most of his comrades were down, and he was somehow alone on the flank. As he turned to move back to his men, he suddenly stood face to face with a Yankee private. He looked into the Yankee's face and thought how much the boy looked like his cousin Calvin back in Cherokee. The sight of the enemy soldier so close to him alarmed him to a great degree. His first reaction was to lunge at the boy with his bayonet. As he thrust the blade at the Yank, the point miraculously drove between the boys arm and his side, completely missing solid flesh. The Yank was as startled as Jedediah and turned to his right and pushed his own bayonet into Jedediah's side. The cold steel sank deep into Jed's loin and he knew instantly he was mortally wounded. The Yank thought best to move quickly away from the conflict and ran back up to the tree line to join his men.

Jedediah lay on the ground for a short spell to assess his predicament. He knew his only chance of living was to move to the rear and find the surgeon's tent and receive treatment for his wound. The smoke from the battle was quite intense, and Jedediah became confused. He moved too far to the east than he should to join up with his fellow Rebs. After what must have been two hours of agonizing travel, Jedediah eased himself up against a large cedar tree and leaned his head back against the trunk to rest. He had a piece of cornbread left from breakfast and a full canteen of water, so he sat a moment and took a bite of the bread and drank deeply from his canteen.

Jed heard a noise to his left and saw a Yankee soldier moving toward him from the tree line. Jed could see the Yankee's left shoulder had been almost blown away, and he saw the boy stagger and almost go to his knees.

"Hey, Yank," Jed yelled. "Come over here and we can die together."

The startled Yankee tried to raise his Springfield rifle to his shoulder but had forgotten that most of the shoulder wasn't there. In inspecting the Rebel, the Yank realized the boy leaning against the tree posed no threat to his safety.

The two men sat for a spell and Jed found out the boy's name was Albert Slocum from Michigan. He had fought at Shiloh and Corinth and never received so much as a scratch. Today his own cannon battery misfired a shell that exploded just to his rear sending blazing metal into his shoulder. He had lain on the battle field unconscious for several hours. Upon awakening, Albert had moved east instead of north.   When he arrived at the cedar thicket, he only had his Springfield with him. He had no knowledge as to where his other belongings were.   Jedediah gave the Yank some water and offered him food. After some time the boy ceased to speak and Jedediah realized Albert had slumped over on the grass and breathed his last. Jed thought of the day when he joined up and the pledge he made to fight and kill as many Yankee`s as he could. Now as he looked at the boy in blue, laying on southern soil in death, he wished in some way he could have helped Albert from Michigan.

Jedediah looked at the sky and knew it must be getting on to about three or four in the afternoon.   The weather had been quite warm for September and he put his blanket and other belongings to his side. He had lost considerable blood and he knew he would not last the day. He thought of home and his mother. He reached inside his pack and pulled out the notebook he had been saving to write of his exploits in battle. He thought he should use it to write his mother. He knew she would never see the letter but somehow he felt God might convey his thoughts to his mother if he wrote them down.   He pulled out us pencil, opened the notebook and wrote.

"To My Dearest Mother—

Chapter 11

We pulled up the barn about dusk and unloaded our tree. Jenny and I didn't speak as we took the harness assembly off Charley and led him to his stall where he immediately went to his oat bag. Jenny took my hand, and we went in to tell Agnes of our experiences of the day.

We told Agnes all the details of the two boys and then showed her the notebook. Jenny placed the notebook in Agnes' hands, and we sat back to see her reaction.

Agnes turned to the opening page and read several lines. She lifted her eyes and looked out the kitchen window toward the corn field. Her mind wandered to earlier days when her own two boys were laughing while they did their work in the field. She thought of the ache still inside her as she missed her boys so terribly. She looked up and spoke to Jenny and me.

"This is the letter of a dying boy to his mother. If someone ever finds a letter my boys had written to me, I would hope they would read it and try to get it to me. We need to know what this boy from Cherokee said to his mother. Maybe we can find her and give her these final words of her son."

Agnes got up from the straight chair at the table and moved to her comfortable chair in front of the fireplace. She raised the wick in the Aladdin Lamp to it's brightest point and started reading the last words of Jedediah Tomkins.

"To My Dearest Mother,

I fear I have distressing news for you. I have been killed today by a Yankee soldier in a battle in Iuka, Mississippi, not too far from our home. I was unfortunate enough to be too close to him when he thrust his bayonet in my side. It hurt grievously for a spell, and then I felt no pain whatever. I have very little of the war to tell you as my time as a fighting man was brief. I fired my gun a few times but doubt I caused any harm to the Yankee army. What I observed today makes me believe we cannot win this war. The Yanks I saw were better trained and much better equipped than our boys. They made short order of our company, and I fear Captain Stevens also met his maker this day.

I wish there were some way I could return to you. I know with daddy's passing and Brother Will leaving to fight in the war, you and Megan are left by yourselves. I feel the toils of the farm will be more than you and sister can endure. I have to pray that God will sustain you.

I know from today that war is a grievous affair. I ask you to plead with cousin Paul to stay home and out of this terrible struggle. I know he is now sixteen and will be wanting to join a regiment and fight for our glorious land.

Today, I met a young Yankee who was from Michigan. His name was Albert. He was a nice enough sort of boy and under other circumstances I feel we could have been friends. He talked a little different, but he, too, was nineteen and wishing he could go back to Michigan to his folks. Albert died by my side in a very peaceful manner.

I wish I had time to tell you more, but I feel I am drifting. I have a peace in my spirit knowing that this will not be the last body I will inhabit. I look forward to seeing you and daddy on the other side in glory. I am weary now and will end this letter.

Your loving son,
Jedediah"

Jenny was crying openly, and I too had tears streaming down my face. Agnes paused after reading the letter and looked into the fire. She didn't speak for several minutes, and then she reached out her hands to Jenny and me. We moved forward on the sofa and each took one of Agnes' hands in ours. Agnes looked into our eyes, and barely holding back the sobs spoke softly.

"I have had a strange feeling these last days and I am now convinced the Lord has placed us in this position to help those in distress. Mr. Lincoln's Gold was meant to pay for men to fight and kill but in God's providence it has fallen into our hands, and I plan for us to use it for good wherever we can. Jedediah mentions the dire straits of his mother and sister in his letter. Somehow the Lord has led you two to the Cedar Grove to find his body and this remarkable letter. I propose you two go to Cherokee and try to find Mrs. Tomkins and deliver her son's letter to her. I also propose that we give her whatever money she needs to keep her on her feet through the winter. She has no man at home, and it will be difficult for her and her daughter to sustain any kind of life for themselves."

Agnes looked again at the letter and then slowly closed the notebook and placed it in my hands. As I looked at the book holding Jedediah Tomkins' letter, I knew Agnes was right. We would never be able to use all of Mr. Lincoln's Gold for ourselves. I had been a member of this family for just a few months and yet I had a feeling we were not people who desired wealth just for the sake of it.

I knew at that moment we had embarked on a grand adventure, ordained by God. I had no idea at that time who we would help with Mr. Lincoln's Gold but I knew if we opened our eyes and our hearts God would guide us.

Jenny and I vowed that night the first day after Christmas we would take the wagon and go to Cherokee, Alabama and find Mrs. Tomkins. Our last question to each other before we drifted off to sleep was how much of Mr. Lincoln's Gold should we give the Tomkins family?

Chapter 12

On Christmas Day we enjoyed a sumptuous family meal. I don't ever remember us celebrating Christmas back in Galena so my time with Jenny and Agnes was special.

The weather was not too cold so we got in the wagon and started toward the cedar grove to place the markers on the boy's graves. Jenny had made some very nice crosses from old barn pieces and put inscriptions on them.

As we stood amidst the thick trees looking at the newly dug graves, we thought again of the two young boys laying cold in the ground at an age when they should be courting and even possibly raising a family. Agnes said some appropriate words, and we placed the crosses at the head of each boy. The first simply said;

ALBERT - A YOUNG BOY
FROM MICHIGAN

The second read;

PRIVATE JEDEDIAH TOMKINS
1ST ALABAMA INFANTRY

We smoothed the dirt on the graves and walked back to the wagon in silence. When we got back to the house, I built a fire, and we sat down to decide on our course of action with regards to Jedediah's mother and sister. I knew we had enough money to get Mrs. Tomkins fixed up for life, but Agnes said we should respect the family and not make them feel like a charity case. Agnes also stressed that if the Tomkins all of a sudden became wealthy it would raise too many eyebrows in the community.

We decided on $2000. We knew with this amount Mrs. Tomkins and her daughter could live nicely during the winter and have ample left over to hire a helper for planting time. Whatever the result, we felt the $2000 would go a long way toward easing the burden of Mrs. Tomkins and her daughter, Megan.

We also knew that regardless of the extra trouble involved it could never be revealed where the money had come from. If word ever got out that Agnes Swanson and her daughter and son- in- law had thousands of dollars, nothing but trouble would occur.

We devised a simple plan. Jenny and I would go to Cherokee and quietly find where Mrs. Tomkins lived. We would make sure Mrs. Tomkins was home and under the cover of darkness leave the bag of money and Jedediah's letter on her porch. Jenny and I would not leave until we knew Mrs. Tomkins had found the letter and the money.

We had heavy rain the Wednesday and Thursday after Christmas, but on Friday the skies cleared and the weather was quite nice. I made a cover for the bed of the wagon, so if we did meet with bad weather, Jenny and I could be quite comfortable bundled up under the canvas. Jenny fixed us three meals for the trip. We didn't know how long it would take to get to Cherokee, but we were prepared to spend one night on the road. Agnes made a sturdy bag with a draw string and we placed two hundred of the Gold Eagles in the bag. I put them under the seat along with our food. Jenny carried Jedediah's letter under her coat. She was more protective of the letter than the gold. Charley seemed to realize we were making a special trip and was very active as I placed the harness around his neck.

The trip to Cherokee was uneventful. We crossed a bridge over Bear Creek and saw three small boys playing on the banks of the small stream. We passed a few homes but encountered no riders or other wagons on the road. The rains had caused deep ruts in places, and I wondered what we would do if we did have to pass another wagon on the small road.

We arrived in Cherokee a little after noon and pulled up to a house just outside the small town. We were determined not to be seen by too many people as we didn't want to cause any concern among the locals. There was a young girl on the porch who looked to be about thirteen but was very alert and quite bright of mind. She said she knew Mrs. Tomkins well. She said word had come that both Mrs. Tomkins' boys were missing in battle and thought dead. She blushed and said she had a crush on Jedediah and told him when he came back from killing Yankees, she was going to marry him. She choked back a tear and pointed to a small road about a hundred yards east. She said that road led to the Tomkins place. We thanked her and urged Charley on down the road.

The road to the Tomkins farm had not had much travel and the ruts were very shallow. As we approached the house we could see a wagon out by a small barn but no horse could be seen at all. Many of the southern men took the family animal with them when they went to war. This appeared to be the case with Jedediah's brother. There was one milk cow grazing behind the barn and smoke was coming from the chimney of the house. The house was one of the dog trot houses I had seen so much around Iuka. There were rooms on both sides with an opening in the center. The idea was the dogs could run through the center whenever they wanted to. I had never been in one of these strange houses, but they looked secure and comfortable. We knew we were at the right place when Jenny found a crude carving on the fence post saying;

GATE BUILT BY WILL TOMKINS - 1859

We remembered Jedediah had mentioned his brother was named Will. There was a good sized pine thicket just south of the house and we had Charley pull the wagon behind two large trees where it couldn't be seen from any direction. I hung the oat bag over Charley's head and he seemed quite content to stand there and munch on his afternoon's rations. Near dark we saw a young woman appear on the porch. We figured it must be Megan, Jedediah's sister. After a short time, a small gray haired lady joined the girl on the porch, and they stood facing the sunset to the west. It was if they were still looking for their men to return at any time.

It must have been near nine o'clock when the lamps were dimmed in the house. I told Jenny we should wait awhile longer before we put the letter and money on the porch as we didn't want to be detected. Jenny had written a note and put it just inside the book. It said,

Dear Mrs. Tomkins,
By chance we came upon the remains of your son and found the enclosed book. It has a letter from him that I know he wanted you to have. We are so sorry about your loss. Please accept the gift of the

enclosed money. It will never replace your son, but maybe it will ease your burdens as you keep up your home place on this lovely hill.

Sincerely,
Concerned friends

JANUARY 1st, 1863– TOMKINS FARM- CHEROKEE, ALABAMA

It had been three days since Megan found the bag of money and the letter from Jedediah. On that cool morning when she went out to sweep the porch she had almost stumbled over the bag lying just outside the front door. At first she thought one of the neighbors had brought by some food, but when she lifted the bag, it was almost more than she could carry.   She took the bag and the book inside and placed them before her mother who was finishing her breakfast coffee at the kitchen table. Megan first opened the bag and poured out the large stack of gold coins. Mrs. Tomkins had seen some gold Eagles at the town store and on one occasion had even seen two Double Eagles. Megan had never seen a gold coin before and wanted her mother to assure her they were real.   Both Tomkins' ladies were stunned. Not until they opened the book and read Jenny's note did they realize that the money was for them.

Times had been hard on the place since the boys left. Will had taken Champ, the family horse with him to the Cavalry when he left home back in March of `61. After Jedediah joined the army last May there was no one to do heavy chores around the small farm.   Megan and Mrs. Tomkins had planted a nice garden, but with no extra cash crops around, the money was almost gone. They had about eighty dollars in Confederate bills, but the local store had quit taking them. Had it not been for the ladies of the local Methodist Church, Megan and her mother would not have had a decent Christmas meal. Mrs. Tomkins told Megan on the Wednesday after Christmas the only hope they had for the immediate future was to try to find a buyer for the farm and maybe move in with her sister in the north end of the county.

A rider had come on Thanksgiving Day with the news about the boys. The letter about Jedediah was from a Colonel Harris stating that Private Jedediah Tomkins had bravely fought in the Battle of Iuka and was missing along with many members of his company. A lengthy search for his body had taken place, and it was now assumed he was killed in the battle and buried by Northern troops. Colonel Harris expressed his extreme regrets to Mrs. Tomkins and assured her the Confederate Army would continue in its quest to rid our land of the aggressors from the North.

The other letter was from General Orville Joseph`s aide saying Sergeant William Tomkins had been killed in a cavalry attack on Union forces just outside Nashville, Tennessee. The letter told of the gallantry under fire of Sergeant Tomkins and how he distinguished himself in battle and fought bravely to the end.

Mrs. Tomkins and Megan were devastated at the news of Will and Jedediah`s deaths. Megan was particularly crushed as her two brothers were her idols. Mrs. Tomkins had somehow known when her boys left they would never return to her. Her grief was deep, but she knew somehow she must carry on.

Mrs. Tomkins read her son`s letter over and over and thanked God every night some Good Samaritan had brought it to her. Having Jedediah`s last written words would mean much to her through the years.

The money was a God Send. With the two thousand dollars, she could buy seed for the crops and pay Simms Adams a decent salary to farm the land for her. Simms was a fifty year old colored man who worked for her husband before the war. Simms loved the farm and would jump at the chance to live in the back room of the barn and work the place. Mrs. Tomkins could buy a decent horse and another cow as well as pigs and chickens. She and Megan would always miss Jedediah and Will, but life on the farm could now be happy again.

At night Mrs. Tomkins would pray to God thanking him for the abundance that had befallen her. She wished she knew who had given her the money but she knew she never would. She thought of one of her mother`s favorite passages of scripture where Jesus said,

"When you have done it unto one of the least of these, my brethren, you have done it unto me."

Martha Tomkins knew somehow her benefactor's had served their Lord in a wonderful way by helping her. She would be eternally grateful.

Chapter 13

Jenny and I saw the girl pick up the bag of coins and the book and go inside the house. We knew our task was complete. We had no way of knowing how the Tomkins' ladies would use the money but it was our deep hope their lives would be better because of it. Jenny moved over close to me on the wagon seat as we started our journey back home. As she put her arms through mine and pulled tight I could feel her love coming through my coat.

We told Agnes of our trip and all that had occurred. Agnes was pleased and had us say a special prayer for Mrs. Tomkins and her daughter before we retired that evening. We had several decisions to make regarding the remaining money, and as I turned away from Jenny during the night I knew that now was the time to move the rest of Mr. Lincoln's Gold.

We made inquiries throughout town about the war, and from the news we received, there was no activity in our area. One salesman told of being in Corinth and seeing the garrison of Union soldiers placed there. Most were camped near the rail crossing and life in the town appeared normal. He reported that in his journey over from Corinth he had not seen any soldiers, Union or Confederate. When we were sure we would have a safe trip to the river we started making plans about the gold. The sheer weight and volume of that much gold would be a problem. Agnes saved all the seed and fertilizer bags from the store, and I started digging more holes out in the edge of the woods. Our house was well situated for privacy. We were nestled in a valley inside three hills with the farm not visible from the main road. We had few visitors, so my work was undetected.

We waited until April when the weather moderated to make our journey. Jenny insisted she accompany me, and I made no objection to it. She could, in fact, be quite a help to me in loading the trunks of gold.

It was a beautiful spring morning when we started our trip to the river. The dogwoods were in full bloom and the hills were white with their open blooms. The air was clean and fresh smelling, and Jenny seemed to love the trip. She had never seen the Tennessee River and was eager to see so large a body of water. When I turned onto the small road leading to the river, I could see there were fresh horse tracks on the path. I urged Charley to a halt and dismounted from the wagon, so I could investigate. As I approached the edge of the river I saw my rock ledge hiding place and could tell it had not been disturbed. I was surprised to see a horse tethered to a tree. On closer investigation, I noticed a boy and girl fishing from the bank of the river. Two cane poles were stuck into the ground, and there were two floats on the surface made from bark off a pine tree. The couple was no more than fifteen feet from the rock ledge where Mr. Lincoln's gold had been resting for over a year.

I certainly had no intention to harm the young boy and girl, so I decided to retreat back to the wagon, move a distance away and wait for them to retire from the area. As I was turning to leave I saw the young man reach his hand under the young ladies full skirt and tilt her back to the ground. I knew far too well his intentions and realized I had no business intruding in the love life of this young Tennessee couple. I quietly made my way back to Jenny and informed her of my findings.

"You mean he actually placed his hand under her skirt right there in the open for God and everyone to see?" said Jenny. "Well, I never heard of such." She didn't know I saw the huge smile on her face.

I laughed and pulled Jenny into my arms. I told her the boy wasn't doing anything he hadn't wanted to do back in Galena when he was that age but never had the gumption to try.

Jenny hit me on the chest and with a large grin on her face said, "I think that's all you men think about. You ought to be ashamed of yourself?"

I kissed Jenny lovingly and had we not had such an important task to fulfill would have done the same thing the young couple was now engaged in.

We urged Charley back up the small road to the main turn and could tell by the tracks the horse had come from the north. We went a few yards south and pulled off the road to wait. I decided if the couple discovered us, I would simply say we were out on a picnic and were headed for the river.

It must have been two hours before we saw the horse and both it's riders enter the main road and turn back north. The girl had her arms firmly around the young man's waist and her head was buried against his back. As the horse turned, we could see a lovely smile on her face.

I never thought of others using the spot there at the river but I now assumed that in the past year many others had been there within arms reach of unbelievable riches. I hoped it was all still intact.

As we pulled up to the rivers edge, we could see a small boat out near the center of the river. The man in the boat was running a trot line, and we saw him place three fish in his boat. As we stood there in this peaceful setting looking at a man doing his daily chores as a fisherman and thinking of the young couple in love, it was hard to imagine that throughout our land young men were fighting and dying in battles so fierce and horrible the mind couldn't imagine.

I directed Jenny to the rock ledge. As I pulled back the branches I could see all the trunks holding Mr. Lincoln's Gold still resting where I had placed them a year ago. Jenny looked at me and gave me that wonderful smile that was all her own.

"What a great hiding place, Marcus", Jenny said. "No one would have ever found the gold."

I had been thinking about it for several months but now as I stood there and looked about me I realized this was the only place up and down this area of the river where the trunks could have been hidden so perfectly. I shared my feelings with Jenny and told her I was certain now a higher being had directed my every move the day of the battle at Pittsburg Landing. It was divine providence that placed the gold in my hands, and this same divine providence took care of it safely here by the river. I told Jenny we had somehow been chosen as God's instruments and it was up to us to make sure Mr. Lincoln's Gold was used to help as many people as possible.

Jenny worked tirelessly as she helped me load the trunks in the wagon. It was getting quite late when we finished. We decided to bed down here by the river for the night and head back to the farm early in the morning. I built a small fire. Jenny opened a can of beans and I cooked a slab of bacon. The meal was quite good and filling. The night was beautiful and as we sat looking at the stars Jenny turned to me, smiled and whispered.

"Now, tell me again, what exactly did that young boy do this afternoon?"

By now I knew Jenny well enough to pick up on an open invitation like that and responded in kind. I never tired of making love to Jenny, but for some strange reason this night was even more special than any before. Maybe it was the open air. Maybe it was the thought of the young couple or maybe it was just God affirming his choice of us as his servants. Whatever the reason, Jenny and I knew this evening would be remembered all our days.

We arrived back at the farm around two o`clock. With Agnes and Jenny helping me we finished our task just before dark. We opened all the trunks, broke them up and burned them. We then took the small boxes of coins and put them in the burlap bags to be buried. We carefully made sure none of the bags were too heavy for Jenny and Agnes to lift. There was always the possibility something could happen to me, and I wanted them to be able to handle the bags by themselves. It took quite a space to bury all the bags, but when we covered the ground with pine needles, you could not tell where the holes had been dug.

As we enjoyed the fried chicken supper Agnes had prepared, I told the ladies how relieved I was to know we no longer needed to worry about having to go back to the river to get the gold. It was now on our property and properly hid. At this point, we had no idea what would come of our efforts, but we all had a peaceful feeling about it.

Agnes turned to Jenny and then looked at me.

"I don`t know what it is but you two look like you are glowing. Why, If I didn`t know better I would think you two were in love."

She laughed out loud as she finished her cup of coffee.

Jenny squeezed my hand under the table, and I could see she was blushing. I think Agnes could tell something special had occurred on our trip to the river.

Chapter 14

Agnes told me the next morning she was concerned all the money was in gold. Sooner or later people were going to wonder that everything we paid for was with gold and not paper money. Agnes said we should start trying to gradually change some of the gold into currency. The local bank still had ample U.S. Currency and was eager to exchange the greenbacks for gold. We were careful not to raise any suspicions by taking too much in at a time. It didn't amount to much, but by April we had several hundred dollars in paper money. The drummer who traveled all around the area agreed to take gold coins to other banks for us. Agnes told the man she had become concerned about having gold around and felt safer with the easier to hide paper money. Since she never sent over eighty to a hundred dollars at a time, the drummer was happy to oblige and never suspected there were thousands of dollars more up in the woods. He started bringing a few twenty dollar bills of his own money and swapping it for the gold Eagles. He said his wife loved the look of the shiny gold coins.

Jenny and Agnes made a point to present a new ten dollar Eagle when purchasing anything from local people. Most were more than glad to give change in silver coins or paper dollars. We readily took Confederate currency as well. I think we all realized that in a short while this Southern Script, as the Yankees called it, would be worthless.

By spring, 1863, travel on the roads was back to normal, and we received week old newspapers from Memphis and Birmingham. As time passed, it was easy to see the tide of battle had turned in favor of the North. In July we received word that General Lee had suffered a tremendous defeat in a small farm town in Pennsylvania named Gettysburg. Just two days later General Grant entered Vicksburg in Mississippi and virtually split the Confederacy in half. A naval fleet had formed a blockade at vital sea ports cutting off any support the south might receive from England. Even the most die hard Rebel faithful in town agreed. Although the war might continue for some time it was now a decided matter. The south would lose this war.

Supplies became harder and harder to get, and by January of 1864 Agnes decided to only open the store three days a week. She could still get a few basics, but sugar, coffee, tea and canned goods became almost non existent. People learned to live almost totally off the land. Our neighbor up the road, Mr. J.H. Ray, had several bee hives and provided us with ample honey. Agnes and Jenny were quite good at using the honey in place of sugar. At first an apple pie sweetened with honey tasted a little funny, but soon we grew to like it. We had two sassafras trees near the fence line and Agnes concocted a nice tasting tea from its sweet smelling roots. We accumulated a good stock of chickens and had ample eggs and an endless supply of small chicks coming along. I fenced in a small section behind the barn, and we kept two hogs fattening up for fall killing time. They made it fine on the scraps from the table and melons we grew in the garden. We got the hogs from our neighbor, Mr. Shepherd. His place wasn`t detected when the battle broke out in Iuka, and he still had his prize stock of pigs. Mr. Shepherd was happy to swap us two small pigs each summer for fresh vegetables from our garden.

An old colored man would bring fresh catfish by about twice a month to exchange for eggs and chickens. I always liked fish and the catfish Agnes cooked was very palatable to the stomach. With fresh onions and cornbread it made for a delicious meal.

Although we had to adapt a little we made it quite well and lived very comfortably on our farm. We found out, however that all our neighbors weren`t as fortunate as we were.

Our good friends, Mr. and Mrs. Adams, had virtually had to close the harness shop. There was simply no business for such items and Mr. Adams got in pretty dire financial straits. Luckily they owned the building the shop was in, and they lived upstairs. Mrs. Adams told Agnes they might have to leave Iuka and go to her father`s home in Holly Springs. With no farm to provide food and no money to purchase supplies, they had very little on the table. Mrs. Adams was also in bad spirits, as she hadn`t heard from her son, Hiram, in some time. Hiram had gone to Union University in Jackson, Tennessee to become a preacher but while there was encouraged to join the

Confederate Army and fight for the south. His regiment had been sent north to fight with General Lee, and it had now been three months since Mrs. Adams received any communication from her son.

JULY 3RD 1863- SECOND TENNESSEE INFANTRY-GETTYSBURG., PA.

Corporal Hiram Adams was bone weary as he made his way to the rendevous point at the corn field. It was now the third day of the Battle of Gettysburg. Hiram and his brigade had participated in two bitter battles the day before as the Second Tennessee supported General Longstreet's Army of the West in their attempt to take the high ground around the small town of Gettysburg in southern Pennsylvania. The Rebels fought bravely, and with vigor, but were repelled each time by fierce cannon and rifle fire from the larger Yankee force firmly entrenched behind well placed wooden emplacements. Casualties were quite heavy, and Corporal Adams saw many of his comrades fall in the battle.

As Hiram approached the open field on the morning of July 3rd he knew that many more would fall this day. His unit was to be on the right flank of the massive force led by General George Pickett. Pickett had been ordered by General Lee to move his entire division across the open field. When reaching the Union lines he was to take and hold the high point securing victory for the South in the battle between Lee's Army of Northern Virginia and General Meade's Army of the Potomac. It would be a glorious undertaking, thought Hiram, and one that would ensure final victory for his beloved South in the battle against the Yankee's from the north.

Hiram and his squad sat beneath two black jack oak trees and ate the last of the biscuits given them before the battle the day before. As Hiram looked around at his friends and fellow soldiers he realized that seven of the original sixteen men who left Union University to fight for the South were no longer there. Six had been killed in action and one, Madison Strickland, died of a severe case of dysentery in April. Of the remaining nine men left only two had not suffered some kind of wound.

Hiram thought back to the night in 1861 when the Captain in the beautiful gray uniform gathered the men together in the chapel at

Union University. The flamboyant Captain gave his dramatic speech as to why they should all leave their studies and join the Confederate Army in it`s struggle against the hated Yankees. Hiram remembered how he had tried to balance his love for his homeland against his love for his Lord and his desire to be a Minister of the Gospel. As he watched the enthusiasm of his friends and fellow students grow he knew he had but one choice and that was to join the Confederate forces.

Hiram and his fifteen friends joined the Captain and became part of the Second Tennessee Infantry Brigade. Captain Brubaker was the son of a wealthy Nashville banker and used his own funds to purchase flashy gold trimmed uniforms for his men. The men were also issued the new Sharp`s rifles and in a short time of intense training became a very competent fighting force. The Second Tennessee performed brilliantly at First Manassas and at Chancellorsville.

Hiram and his friends had long since disposed of the original fancy gray uniforms and acquired more practical and comfortable clothing better suited to the rigors of battle. As Hiram looked at the eight friends around him who had become closer than brothers, he saw little that would remind him of the smooth faced boys from college. These were bearded, hardened veterans of events no young man should ever see, let alone participate in. Hiram lost count of the men he had killed in battle. He remembered the first man he shot at Manassas and the strange look on the face of the young Yankee as he slumped to the ground in death. Hiram somehow made himself believe what he was doing was right and if he had to kill to secure the proper end to this struggle then so be it. Hiram`s thoughts turned to his home and family.

Hiram longed to see his mother and father back in Iuka, Mississippi. He wished for the fellowship of the First Baptist Church and all the loving people that meant so much to him as he had grown up in his home town. He knew the only way he could return to them would be to help win this war.

Captain Brubaker told the men last night of their assignment for this day. He said they would be in the most strategic location on the battlefield and would need to use all their training and bravery to succeed. Captain Brubaker told of actually seeing General Lee at the briefing for the battle and how impressed he was with the great General.

General Pickett arrived at full sunlight and rode up and down the lines encouraging all the boys and promising them victory before this day was over. The men seemed secure in their leader and anticipated a great fight. The entire division of fifteen thousand men roared into action as the General led the way.

The enemy cannon started their barrage as the corps reached the middle of the open field. The blasts were so numerous there were no silent moments between them. Captain Brubaker fell in the first outburst and one shell hit ten feet to Hiram's left cutting Wilbert Hawkins in half. Stuart Johnson also fell with the side of his face taken off. Hiram continued moving forward and heard the sound of intense rifle fire. The brigade was now in range of the Yankee rifles and the puffs of smoke they made as they fired was so great the trees were soon blocked from view.

Men were falling as they ran forward and yet the column of gray continued to move on. As they had been trained, the boys closed ranks to fill in the gaps as men fell. Hiram felt a slap on his right arm and realized a minnie ball had pierced his shirt sleeve but had not touched flesh. His fellow soldiers stopped their customary yelling and were simply trying to stay alive as they moved forward. The cannons started firing with regularity again causing terrible carnage as the shells struck their marks. Officers and their men were falling all around Hiram but the orders were to advance forward.

Hiram faced heavy fire at Chancellorsville and was in close hand to hand combat at Manassas but what he was experiencing at this moment was far worse than anything he had ever known. He had stepped off the face of the earth and landed in Sheol. The smell was a combination of smoke and body parts and excrement. Hiram could see the column had crossed the field and was now starting it's ascent up he hill. The cannon fire abated but the rifle fire became, if anything, more intense. When it appeared the gray line might succeed in breaching the crest more intense fire met them as Yankee reserves moved forward to join the fray.

General Pickett had but one course of action. He realized the day was lost and ordered his men to retire to the rear. As Hiram turned to follow his comrades he felt a searing blow to his back and neck. He had been struck by two separate minnie balls and fell to the ground. The last thing he said before he died was, "Mother."

Of the fifteen thousand men who started across the field behind General Pickett, less than five thousand would return to fight again. The Second Tennessee Infantry Brigade suffered over eighty per cent casualties. Of the sixteen men who left Union University in 1861 to fight for the Confederacy not one would return. The last remaining nine men were all killed in Pickett's charge at Gettysburg on July 3rd, 1863.

Chapter 15

It was late September before the news of Hiram`s death arrived in Iuka.   A civilian from Corinth brought a casualty report from Gettysburg that had been in the Nashville Banner in August. He had seen the name Hiram Adams in the paper and knew of Mr. and Mrs. Adams in Iuka. He felt the need to make the day long journey from Corinth to tell them of their son`s death.  He had also been given a letter to bring to the Adams family that had been written by one of Hiram`s commanding officers. The letter had been written in July but had just now reached the rail station in Corinth with other mail from the north. The letter said,

Dear Mr. and Mrs. Adams,
I regret to inform you that your son, Corporal Hiram Adams was killed in the Battle of Gettysburg in Pennsylvania. Corporal Adams fought bravely and honored your name and his homeland with his dedication and devotion to duty.   General Lee sends his condolences and hopes your grief can be tempered by knowing what a fine and gallant soldier your son, Hiram was.
Your faithful servant,

Colonel B.F. Lee,
Army of Northern Virginia

A memorial service was held for Hiram at the First Baptist Church in Iuka. Several people spoke including former Sunday School teachers and classmates. A young lady described Hiram as the one the other kids in school looked up to. I wish I had known Hiram Adams. He was just one year older than I and from all the things I heard of him, I know we would have been friends. Jenny said he was sweet, quiet, good looking, patient and very religious. She said he never wanted to be anything but a preacher. What a shame he had to take arms against other young men and kill and finally be killed.

Mr. and Mrs. Adams were quite brave. Hiram was their only child and it was if they had given him up when he left home back in `61.

Mrs. Adams was obviously touched by the support of her church friends and she held up nicely during the service.

Agnes said she was concerned about the day to day welfare of Mr. and Mrs. Adams. She felt it was time for Mr. Lincoln's Gold to be used again to help a needy friend. While the Adams were eating supper with their cousins down the street, Jenny and I placed a bag of coins in their parlor with a short note attached. It simply said,

To special people. Your son honored all with his life and service to his country. May this token of appreciation help ease your grief and make your life easier.
Loving friends.

When Mr. and Mrs. Adams found the bag of coins they poured them out on their kitchen table and counted them. The total came to two thousand dollars. As they read the letter tears poured down their cheeks. Mr. Adams knew that with this sum they would be secure for the rest of the war. They would somehow make a comeback in the business once this horrible conflict was over.

Mrs. Adams asked her husband where the money had come from. He told her he had no idea but as he lay in bed that night he tried to imagine who would have this kind of money to give and who would have been so generous with it. He knew he would never mention it, but the only person in the world who would have done such a thing if she had the means would have been Agnes Swanson. Before he went to sleep he thanked God for his son, his wife and dear friends. He mentioned one by name. Agnes.

The war lasted almost two more years and on April 9th, 1865 General Robert E. Lee surrendered to General Ulysses S. Grant in the courthouse at Appomattox, Virginia. The conflict that had started in 1861 saw over six hundred thousand Americans killed on both sides.

Mr. Lincoln was murdered soon after the war ended.

In the years from 1863 to the end of the war Jenny and I placed Mr. Lincoln's Gold in the hands of numerous families, businesses and churches. Most gifts ranged from five hundred dollars to the five thousand dollars we left at the altar of the Christ Methodist Church after fire destroyed a large part of their building. We estimated we still had well over four hundred thousand buried on the farm. We knew that although the war was over hard times would be ahead for a lot of people. We decided to live as normal lives as possible and wait for divine providence to lead us in the use of Mr. Lincoln's Gold.

Jenny presented me with a fine son on Christmas Day 1866. We named him Jedediah Albert Wade after the two boys we buried in the cedar thicket back in `62. We decided to call our son Jed. By the time he was ten, Jed could plow a mule, weed the garden, and put a harness on our new horse, Jude. Charley had gotten gimpy in the legs, and we let him wander in the pasture to his hearts content. Charley had served us well, and it was now his time to enjoy what life he had left. Jake, our mule was still as friendly as ever and never seemed to mind the plow when called upon. Jed loved the farm and I made it a point to try to teach him all I could about the beauty of nature and our responsibility to love and protect the land.

For some reason Jenny never conceived again. We would have liked a girl, but we never questioned the fact we only had one child. He was special and provided us untold hours of love and joy.

Although money wasn't an issue for us, Agnes threw herself into the operation of the store as if she were a teenager. Mr. and Mrs. Adams never got over the grief of losing their son and had moved to Tupelo after the war to live with Mrs. Adams' sister. Before they left they sold Agnes their building and remaining stock of harnesses, saddles, plows and tools. Agnes also purchased the old saloon building on the corner and now had the entire west side of the square for her expanding businesses. She added a full line of feed, seeds and paint. Jed loved working for his grandmother after school each day. I preferred the farm and was happy for him to do what he really liked.

Agnes hired many of the returned soldiers after the war and paid them far more than the jobs were worth. The men felt needed and were thankful to have employment. Swanson's Emporium, as the conglomeration of stores was called in 1883, was the largest retail business in Tishomingo County, Mississippi.

Chapter 16

We decided to tell Jed about Mr. Lincoln`s Gold  the night he graduated from Iuka High School.  He was the same age I was when I got the money and he needed to know the full story.  Agnes made some gingerbread, Jed`s favorite dessert, and we all sat in the soft chairs in front of the fireplace.

I stood and walked to the mantel. I turned and faced Jed. I told him we had something important to tell him. I think Jed thought his mother was going to have another baby. He grinned and put his arm around her shoulders and pulled her close.

I smiled at Jed and began my story. I started from the beginning at Galena, Illinois and made a point not to leave out a single detail. When I got to the part of joining the Union Army, Jed removed his arm from his mother`s shoulder and leaned forward in the seat.  His demeanor changed as he listened carefully to every detail of my story. I told of the battle at Pittsburg Landing and finding  the gold in the wagon.  Jed`s eyes widened when I mentioned the gold.   I continued until I completed the entire story. Jed remained silent as if in a trance.

Jenny stood and picked up the story at the time we found the two dead soldiers in the cedar thicket and buried them. She told how we decided to use the gold to help people in need and that the first person we carried money to was Jedediah Tomkins` mother and sister in Cherokee, Alabama.

Agnes told Jed he had been named for the two boys in those graves. One a southern soldier, and one a young man from the north.

Jed looked at his grandmother, then his mother and finally at me. He stood, walked to the front door and gazed outside. He turned and looked me squarely in the eyes,

"You mean you were a Yankee soldier?" he asked.

"Yes, son I was. I soon realized, however that I could never willfully kill another man and when I had the opportunity to get away from the war, I took it," I answered. "The money was just a stroke of luck. I had no way of knowing what was in that wagon when I jumped in it and raced away."

"If the Yankee`s ever find out who you are and what you did, they`ll shoot you as a thief and a deserter," Jed said, with a forlorn look on his face.

"That`s why we can never tell a soul," said Agnes, breaking into the conversation. "Your daddy is the finest man I have ever known, and he loves you with all his heart. What he did was right, and you must support him in it."

Jed opened the front door and walked out on the porch. He had just heard things he couldn`t believe and couldn`t immediately work out in his mind. We decided to let him think about it for a spell and hope he could accept things as they had to be. It must have been twenty minutes when he came back in the front door, walked over to me and reached out his arms to pull me close. I knew by the look on his face he had accepted his lot in life and would never betray our secret.

"I love you pop, and I am proud of you. Most men would have taken that money and spent it all by now. Your secret is my secret, and whatever I can do to help you just let me know."

We all gathered in a circle of love and I prayed a silent prayer thanking God for giving me this fine young man as my son. As we parted, Jed turned to me and with a big grin on his face said, "Can I see some of Mr. Lincoln`s Gold?  I don`t even know what that much money would look like."

We had a good laugh, and spent the rest of the evening with Jed asking me question after question about my past.

Early the next morning Jed and I went out to the tree line and dug up one of the bags of gold.   I opened a box of coins and handed him a bright shiny ten dollar gold Eagle.

"Here, son. Keep this in a safe place to remind you of the good fortune we have. You will be aiding me from now on as we try to help those people who really need it."

Jed didn`t say anything as we walked back to the house. He flipped the Eagle over and over and finally placed it on his dresser next to his bed. At that moment I knew my son had become a man.

Jed`s first experience as a Good Samaritan was in July when we took $500 in coins and left them at widow Shanks` house. Mrs. Shanks was a nice lady in our church who lost one son at Chattanooga. Another son died of complications from dysentery in a hospital in Virginia. Jenny said she heard the ladies say the Shanks' house was leaking badly, and Mrs. Shanks didn't have the two hundred dollars to pay to have it fixed. We thought we would give her a little extra to tide her over the summer. Jenny let Jed put the bag of coins on Mrs. Shanks' porch late one hot night when we were sure she had gone to sleep. We could tell Jed was pleased with what we had done that night, and I knew then he would make many such trips in the future.

Jed had no desire for college. He loved the stores and felt he was better suited as a merchant than a farmer. He was smart as a whip and was of tremendous help to his grandmother and mother. His knowledge of ciphering and his way with people made him an ideal businessman.

Jed married his high school sweetheart, Molly Thomas, in the spring of 1884. They moved into the well appointed living quarters over the old Harness Shop where Mr. and Mrs. Adams had lived. Jed liked being near the businesses and was downstairs by seven each morning when all the help arrived. Jed held a short meeting with the other men each morning. Although they were all older than Jed and were veterans of the war, they soon realized Jed was very competent in business matters and knew very well what he was doing.

Agnes and Jenny still came in regularly and worked out of the original Swanson's Mercantile building. Jed asked Mark Lockhart to work with Agnes and Jenny. Mark took a minnie ball to his leg at Brice's Crossroads and had a decided limp. Mark carried many ghosts in his mind and was quiet of demeanor. He rarely spoke unless he was spoken to. In the nineteen years Mark had been in Iuka, he rarely ever left the center of town. He ate all his meals at the small café across the street and was friendly to Wanda, the owner. He never went out with her or any other woman in all the intervening years. Jed never questioned Mark about his service in the war. He had a feeling Mark wanted to be left alone. He did his job well, but it was easy to see his past haunted him.

JUNE 10, 1864- 2nd TENNESSEE CAVALRY--BATTLE OF BRICE'S CROSSROADS- NORTHEASTERN MISSISSIPPI

Captain Mark Lockhart got his orders directly from General Forrest. The 2nd Tennessee Cavalry was to lead the main attack against General Samuel Sturgis` Union infantry column encamped on the bank of Tishomingo Creek in Northeastern Mississippi. 2nd Tennessee had distinguished itself admirably in several engagements with General Nathan Bedford Forrest and his famed Cavalry unit.

Captain Lockhart had risen through the ranks from sergeant, then Lieutenant, and now Captain. General Forrest recognized Lockhart`s bravery and horsemanship in raids on Union supply depots in western and central Tennessee. In one particular raid when he was a Sergeant, Mark Lockhart single handedly disrupted a Union encampment of more than twenty Yankee soldiers and occupied them long enough for his unit to confiscate three wagons full of vital food and supplies. Lockhart took a saber slash across his left arm but never wavered in his relentless attack. After the skirmish when Sergeant Lockhart was receiving attention to his wounds at the regiment aid station, General Forrest himself entered the medical tent and personally congratulated Sergeant Lockhart. He promoted him to Lieutenant there on the spot. That was in 1862. Late in `63 when Cavalry Captain Bill Carroll was killed at Collierville, Tennessee, General Forrest promoted Lockhart to Captain and placed him in charge of his best company of riders.

Mark Lockhart was born to be a Cavalry officer. He was raised on a small farm outside Jackson, Tennessee and had been an expert horseman since he was a small boy. His father had trained his son well in the handling and care of horses, and it was only natural that Mark joined the Cavalry when war broke out in 1861. Mark was, at twenty six, a little older than most of the other young recruits trained by General Bedford Forrest`s contingent. He was selected Company Corporal in the first six weeks. He could ride like the wind and had learned to fire his Colt revolver with deadly accuracy. His handling of a saber astounded even his West Point trained instructors.

Mark married Margaret Ray, his childhood companion and the only girl he had ever loved. They had one boy and one girl. Mark and Margaret moved to a forty acre place near Selma, Tennessee and were successful in operating a horse farm. Mark thought this would be his life's work. He heard rumors of war but thought he and his family would never be a part of it. This all changed when Fort Sumter was attacked and war broke out.

Mark's reputation as a horseman had followed him to Selma. In the Spring of '61 he was visited by representatives of General Forrest's Cavalry Corps. Mark was a southerner through and through, and it took little encouragement for him to answer the call to duty.

Captain Mark Lockhart thought of those carefree days back in Jackson and Selma, and he often thought of his wife and children. He knew the only way he would ever be able to return to his past life would be to drive the Yankee invaders from southern soil.

Captain Lockhart led B Company past Brice's Crossroads. As he turned west he saw the large blue column of Yankee infantry encamped by the creek. He didn't hesitate. He ordered his men to charge. His expertly trained and well mounted Cavalry veterans made short work of their task. In less than fifteen minutes they killed or wounded two hundred of the enemy while suffering only nine casualties. The Union soldiers on foot were no match for the charging horsemen. Captain Lockhart realized the day was over for this group of Yankees and ordered his men to retire to join Major J.H. Washburn in a concerted attack on the larger Union column to the west of the creek.

The battle was fierce throughout the day. General Sturgis gathered his remaining Union forces and formed a defensive position in a grove of oak trees. Fighting was intense and Captain Lockhart's unit lost seven more brave men. General Sturgis would lose over twenty six hundred of his Union soldiers that day while General Forrest's casualties were less than five hundred. The battle was a total victory for General Forrest and his men.

As the units were gathering for withdrawal, a wounded Union private raised up from his prone position and fired one last shot from his Springfield rifle before he fell dead on the ground. The bullet struck Captain Mark Lockhart in the leg between the hip and the knee driving deep inside the skin and muscle and shattering the leg bone. Captain Lockhart looked at his leg in astonishment and made his way to the surgeons tent. He fell from his horse unconscious. Two of his comrades eased him to the ground and rushed him inside the temporary hospital.

The Chief Surgeon worked for some time to stop the bleeding and finally had to burn the wound with a hot iron. Just at dusk General Forrest came inside the tent and told the surgeon he wanted Captain Lockhart to live and to live with his leg. He ordered the surgeon to put down his amputation equipment and make sure the leg stayed intact.

Captain Lockhart was sent with other wounded to the hospital in Memphis where he languished between life and death for months. When the war ended in 1865, Captain Lockhart was released from the hospital and told to go home. He was alive but would always walk with a decided limp. It was difficult for him to ride, but his former skills returned enough for him to mount his horse and return to his home in Selma.

Tragedy would meet Captain Lockhart when he arrived at his home place. He found his house burned to the ground and his wife and children buried in graves by the garden. Watson, an elderly colored man was there tending the graves. Watson had worked for Mark and his family before the war. He told Mark a ghastly story. The month before the war ended a group of Union deserters from Corinth raided the farm. They took all the animals and food and burned the house to the ground. Some of the men ravaged Margaret while the two children watched. They shot Margaret and her two children. The deserters left them lying in the dust and rode east toward Birmingham.

Watson had seen these awful events from his shack on the hill. He had immediately buried Margaret and the children.

When Mark made his way to Jackson to check on his parents, he found they had both died of influenza a year ago. The farm was now occupied by Union Army officers who were sent to the area to keep order after the war.

Mark Lockhart was devastated. His life as he had known it was over. He moved from place to place doing odd jobs for food and met a man who told of a lady in Iuka, Mississippi who was offering Confederate veterans jobs. He met Agnes Swanson and her family and became a helper in their retail business. He was given a place to live in the back of the old saloon building that now served as the feed and seed store. Life meant little to Mark Lockhart, but Mrs. Swanson and her grandson, Jed, were kind to him. He became quite good at what he was asked to do around the stores. As the highest ranking officer from the war, Mark Lockhart was looked up to by the other veterans working for Agnes Swanson. Mark made sure the other men earned the gold coins paid them by Mrs. Swanson once a week.

Chapter 17

Word came to Agnes about the terrible state of affairs of Eb Cayson and his family. Eb was a kind Negro man who had been a customer of Agnes and her husband for years. He raised corn and peaches on his place near Burnsville store. The twenty acres had been left to him by his daddy years before. Eb had been friendly with whites all his life. His wife, Ella was a well skilled mid-wife. Ella helped Agnes deliver Jenny back in `42 and had remained Agnes` friend. Since the war ended bad things had been happening out at the Cayson place. One night the barn burned. When the family came home from church one morning, a blazing cross was found in the yard of their house. Word spread that anyone buying corn or peaches from Eb Cayson would be dealt with in a harsh manner.   Eb`s income almost totally stopped as people in the area were terrified of angering the  Ku Klux Klan.   He planted a garden and raised a few chickens, but the Klan made regular visits to his place and destroyed the garden and any livestock left on the place.  Signs were left in the Cayson`s yard demanding they leave the area and go north where they belonged.

I had heard of the Klan activities by stories picked up from drummers and other travelers. It was hard to imagine men so cruel as to cause distress to helpless Negro families who had done nothing of importance in the war. Most of the Negroes I met around Iuka were decent, God fearing folk who meant no harm to anyone. I had met Eb Cayson on several occasions and found him to be a good family man and a man of his word.

Agnes, Jenny, Jed, Molly and I all assembled out at the farm to discuss the plight of the Cayson family and to decide how we could help them. It was clear to all that any money or supplies left at the Cayson farm would be taken by the Klan.

Agnes suggested two plans. First, they would take much needed food and clothing to the Cayson`s immediately. They would then ask Eb and his wife to come in to Iuka to discuss their future. Agnes told of twenty acres of land north of the tree line that was owned by the Bank of Iuka. She suggested using some of Mr. Lincoln's Gold to buy that land and build Eb and his family a nice house and barn on the property. Eb could raise his corn on this land and be protected from the Klan by living so close to the Swanson farm. The only access to Eb's new land would be through Agnes' property. No one dare tread on property belonging to Mrs. Agnes Swanson, Tishomingo County's most successful business person, and a loyal southerner.

Jed talked to Jubal Stokes, one of the veterans who worked in the feed and seed store, about moving out to Eb's place at Burnsville and keep watch over the place. Jubal married Susan Parks and they had three children. The Stokes family had been living in a small house behind the store, and they were quite cramped in their accommodations. Jed knew he could replace Jubal at the store and felt Jubal would jump at the chance to live in a larger house and in the open spaces away from town.

At first Eb said he couldn't leave his daddy's land. When Agnes and I pushed the issue of the Klan and the danger his entire family faced Eb relented. The move to Iuka didn't have to be permanent. When the Klan tired of their efforts Eb could always move back to his home place and Jubal Stokes and his family could take over the twenty acres joining Agnes' land. Eb had met Jubal at the store and the two had become more than speaking acquaintances. Jubal had no animosity toward Negroes and was pleased to call Eb Cayson his friend. Jubal was happy at the thought of going out to the Cayson place and Eb felt well knowing Jubal and his family would be protecting his home and peach orchards.

The necessary transactions were made with the bank. Agnes paid the $1,100 due on the twenty acres of land, and the people at the bank made no special notice that Mrs. Swanson paid the bill with ten dollar Gold Eagles. They just assumed with Mrs. Swanson's successful businesses she was in position to pay that much and more. Arrangements were made with Puckett's Lumber Company to deliver the necessary materials to the new acreage, and Mr. Puckett was more than happy to receive the $1,200 in gold coins to cover the cost of lumber, nails, roofing and paint.

Workers were abundant and by offering $3.00 a day wages it was easy to get the men required to build the house and barn. The work was completed in less than six weeks and by September, 1884, Eb Cayson and his wife and family became our neighbors.

It was a time of transition for the Cayson's, but the peace of mind knowing they would not be bothered by the Klan anymore made up for the sorrow of leaving family land. Eb knew Jubal Stokes would take good care of his home and property at Burnsville. He threw himself into the task of making his new home the best possible for his family. He had adequate land for his corn crop and plenty of space for a good garden. Agnes and Jenny brought them a good brood stock of chickens, and by October they were already gathering eggs and welcoming new chicks to the farm. Jed and I picked up three small pigs from Mr.Shepherd for Eb to raise. The creek just north of the land was full of catfish and carp, so Eb and his boys not only enjoyed the fishing, but provided another good choice of food for the family. By Christmas of `84 Eb Cayson had his new farm going quite nicely.

Eb and his family were no longer bothered by outsiders and were left alone to carve out a new life for themselves under the watch care of their patron saint, Agnes Swanson, and some vital help from Mr. Lincoln.

Jubal and Susan Stokes and their three children moved into Eb Cayson's house next to the peach orchards the first week of October. Jubal was a child of the land and the feel of the open air and the smell of fresh dew on the ground helped Jubal forget the personal tragedies of his past.

Jubal Stokes was a decorated Confederate hero, and when word of his move to the peach orchards spread throughout the area the raids by the Klan ceased.

MAY 2nd, 1863- BATTLE OF CHANCELLORSVILLE, VIRGINIA 3RD INFANTRY CORPS- ARMY OF NORTHERN VIRGINIA

Lt. Jubal Stokes led his 2nd Company of the 3rd Infantry Corps toward Chancellorsville in support of General T.J. Jackson's march against the Union center commanded by General Joe Hooker.

General Hooker entered Virginia by crossing the Rapidan and was moving to trap General Lee and his Army of Northern Virginia before the Confederates could mass an attack on the north. General Lee divided his forces and moved against the Union Army from three directions. Lee's strategy surprised the Union generals and forced them into a defensive position at Chancellorsville. General Lee sensed the advantage and had General Jackson drive his entire corps against the Union line. The initial thrust by the Rebel troops pushed the Union forces almost to the river where they made a brave and gallant stand. After several hours of fierce fighting the battle came to a standstill.

Lt. Jubal Stokes sensed that a move must be made to regain the South's advantage. With saber held high he ordered his men to charge the Union lines. General Jackson observed the action from his position on the crest of a hill and turned to his aide, Colonel Frank Riley.

"Look how that boy fights, Colonel. We can't let him do it all by himself. Send the other lads into the fray. We must have victory by dusk."

The sudden onslaught by the Rebel infantry and cavalry overwhelmed the Union line, and they moved to the rear.

On a reconnaissance the night of the great battle, General Jackson was mortally wounded by his own men. On the next morning, General J.E.B. Stuart took over Jackson's command. He joined the 4th Corps of the Army of Northern Virginia and drove the Union forces from their lines and forced them to retire the battle. General Hooker ordered his entire Union army to cross the Rappahannock at midnight and moved out of Virginia.

General T.J. [Stonewall] Jackson died of his wounds causing General Lee to say,

"I have lost my best friend and my right arm."

On the Monday morning after the battle at Chancellorsville, General Jeb Stuart presented the Confederate Order Of Merit to Lt. Jubal Stokes for his bravery and actions in the battle.

Jubal Stokes would follow General Lee to Gettysburg where he again distinguished himself and received a commendation from the great General himself. Stokes was with the Army of Northern Virginia when Lee surrendered to General Grant at Appomattox. Lieutenant Stokes stayed some time in Virginia to assure that his men had enough supplies to get them home.

Jubal Stokes was born and reared on a farm in Georgia not too far from Atlanta. It wasn't a large place but to Jubal it was heaven on earth. He loved everything about the farm. His daddy had done a good job in preparing and keeping the land through the years. Since the time Jubal turned twelve he became child of the land and a vital part of the overall operation of the farm.

When war broke out, Jubal felt the need to join up and do what he could to help win the war for the south. He had read with interest about General Robert E. Lee, and he desired to serve with the great General. He took his favorite horse and made the long ride to Virginia. Jubal enlisted in the army in Richmond on September of 1861 and was assigned to the 3rd Infantry Corps. He was soon to meet his Commander and mentor, General J.T. Jackson. The General took the boy under his wings and in less than eighteen months Jubal Stokes was in command of a full company of regulars, holding the rank of 1st Lieutenant.

Jubal Stokes was a saddened man when he said goodbye to the men he had served with for four years but he and his men held their heads high. They had done their best for their country and on many occasions had caused the Union forces untold grief. As Jubal mounted his horse for the ride home his ragged, ill equipped men stood at attention and saluted until Jubal was out of sight. It was difficult for Lt. Stokes to hold back the tears.

What Jubal Stokes was to find when he arrived back in Georgia was misery and despair. The land looked as if Satan himself had blown fire across it. In his infamous March to the Sea, General William Tecumseh Sherman had literally obliterated all crops, buildings and livestock from the land. It was difficult for Jubal to determine where his house had been as he looked across the fields of his family's property. He heard from neighbors that his family had literally starved to death the previous winter. When he went into the county seat at Dawsonville, he heard more disturbing news. He no longer owned the land. His family had not been able to pay the taxes on the farm, and it had been taken over by the bank. Northern carpet baggers had bought up most of the farm land in the county by simply paying the unpaid taxes.

Jubal was crushed. He now had no family, no land, no money, and no hope of making any. He asked around for a few weeks but work was not to be had. Word was that Atlanta was in total disarray and confusion and veterans of the war were begging on the streets. He heard from an old friend that if he could get to Memphis, jobs were plentiful on the river front loading and unloading cargo. He knew nothing about this kind of work but wasn't going to stay in Georgia and starve.

His long journey took him across Alabama and into northern Mississippi. He did odd jobs for food on his journey and had been able to kill an occasional squirrel and rabbit to keep him going. He was in a bad state when he entered the small town of Iuka in northeastern Mississippi. He noticed a small café on the square and upon entering asked the young lady at the counter if he could wash dishes for some food.

Susan Parks had seen several of these former soldiers come through town since the war ended the previous April, but this young man was different. Susan couldn't put her finger on it, but she somehow knew this bearded and dirty former soldier standing before her was special. She placed a plate of bacon and eggs before the young man and could tell by his reaction that this was the first food he had eaten in several days.

When Jubal finished his food, he thanked the young lady and asked her what he could do around the place to pay for such a fine meal. Susan told the stranger she was happy to give him the food.

She asked him if he would like to rest and take a bath in her place behind the store next door. Jubal looked into the eyes of the young girl and knew she was an angel from heaven. He gratefully accepted her offer.

Susan put the closed sign on the café window and carried Jubal to her small house next door. She prepared a hot tub of water for him out on the back porch. The August morning was quite warm and Jubal was very comfortable in the open air of the porch. Susan hung a blanket on a clothesline to give the young man privacy.

As Jubal was bathing, Susan thought she would wash his clothes for him. She opened his saddle bag to see if he had an extra shirt to be cleaned. When she raised the flap on the outside pouch, she saw a beautiful blue and gold medal with an attached document. She turned to make sure Jubal couldn't see her. She could hear him splashing in the tub. She unwrapped the document and read it.

"Presented to Lieutenant Jubal Stokes, on this the 6th day of May in the year of our Lord 1863, the Order of Merit of the Confederate States of America. For bravery and valor unsurpassed at the Battle of Chancellorsville, I present to Lieutenant Stokes this highest token of honor given by our beloved Confederacy. In the face of sure death, Lieutenant Stokes, on two occasions, charged the enemy position causing disruption and chaos to their defensive lines. Because of his brave actions, a great victory was secured. As his supreme commander, I commend him and thank him for showing the highest caliber of leadership at a strategic time in the battle."

The commendation was signed by General Robert E. Lee.

Susan carefully placed the commendation and medal back in the saddle bag and realized the man on her back porch was indeed special. She could only imagine what had happened to bring him to such a low point in his life.

After his bath and shave, Jubal sat with Susan on the porch and the two introduced themselves to each other. Jubal told of the destruction of his home property. He told Susan he was on his way to Memphis seeking work. He didn't mention his heroism in the war.

Susan told Jubal she had been widowed in the war before she was nineteen. She had married her high school sweetheart, and he had been killed in the first battle of Manassas back in 1861. She had no family around and had taken the job at the café three years ago. The café owner, Mrs. Stroud, provided her with this small house to live in and gave her ten dollars a week plus her food.   Susan said she had been lucky to get the generous offer.

The two found out they were about the same age. Jubal was twenty four and Susan was twenty three.

The longer the two young people talked the easier it became. Both felt very comfortable with the other and each knew something special had happened that hot morning in August.

Susan told Jubal that Mrs. Swanson was giving former soldiers jobs at her large stores next door to the café. Susan carried Jubal over to meet Mrs. Swanson, and she hired him on the spot. She offered him twenty five dollars a week. Jubal couldn't believe he would receive this small fortune from someone he had never met.

Jubal became quite good at store keeping. He was a natural for the feed and seed store and in less than a year Agnes raised his salary to thirty five dollars weekly. Jubal and Susan fell in love and married in April of `66. They didn't have their first child until the summer of 1871 but had two more in less than four years. In time Jubal let Susan tell all their friends about his medal and commendation. She loved showing it off, especially the signature of General Robert E. Lee.

It wasn't farming but Jubal Stokes had found a home and family. He never quite understood how Mrs. Swanson could pay him and the other men that worked for her the amount of money she did but he accepted it with gratitude.

Jubal noticed that Mrs. Swanson had another unusual habit. She always paid the men in Gold Eagles and one dollar gold coins.

Chapter 18

On Christmas day, 1890, we not only celebrated the birth of Jesus but Jed's birthday as well. As I looked at Jed with his wife Molly, I realized what a fine and outstanding man he was. At twenty four he was far wiser than men twice his age. He had done a wonderful job with all the Swanson stores. They were making quite a nice profit. Of course, the large salaries he was paying the nine employees really came from Mr. Lincoln and not from the store. Even without Mr. Lincoln's gold the stores would have done well. Jed was a natural businessman. He seemed to know the proper things to buy and in the right quantity. People from as far away as Corinth to the west and Savannah to the north knew of Swanson's Emporium in Iuka. They made at least one annual trek to the small town in North Mississippi to stock up on quality, well priced goods. All the local farms bought their seed and fertilizers at Swanson's, and the new paint line Jed put in back in '87 was selling faster than he could keep it on the shelves. The Harness Shop Agnes bought from Mr. and Mrs. Adams was flourishing. Leather goods were now plentiful and Jed had purchased a deluxe line of fine saddles, including the new rage, side saddles for ladies.

Jed purchased the café on the corner in 1888 and employed Robert Forster and his wife to run the place. Jed met Robert and Eileen at a church social and found they had no permanent place to live. For several years they had moved from town to town seeking full time employment. Robert fought with General A. P. Hill during the war. He was like most of the Confederate veterans who were left without a home or gainful employment when the war ended. Robert was forty five years old when Jed hired him to run the café. Robert and Eileen realized Jed's offer of a job was a gift from heaven. They threw themselves into the work with vigor and made the café the stopping off place for all travelers and locals. Eileen was an excellent cook and gained a reputation for her wonderful home made pies and cakes.

As Agnes had done before, Jed paid the Forster`s much more than the job was worth. Jed figured since Mr. Lincoln was footing the bill, why not make Robert`s and Eileen`s life as comfortable as possible. On each Saturday evening Jed would bring four ten dollar Gold Eagles to the café to give to Eileen. It was a fortune to two people who had nothing else of their own.

Each time I went into town, I made it a point to eat at the café. Robert and Eileen were wonderful people and made all customers at the café feel special. As I looked into the faces of the Forster`s it made me extremely proud of Jed and what he had done for their lives.

Jed and Molly presented us our first grandchild, Jedediah, Jr., in the spring of 1886. Laura Bell was born the next year in the fall. Laura Bell was named for Molly`s mother, Laura, and her favorite aunt, Bell. Jed still liked living in town and had the workers add two rooms to the back of his place over the Harness Shop. Walter Sloan, the very first veteran Agnes hired after the war was quite adept with pipes and rigged up running water for Jed and Molly. He somehow got the water to run from a wooden tank beside the well to the sinks in the house. It was ingenious and gave Molly the first running water in town.

Walter lost a leg at the 2nd Battle of Corinth in 1862, and it was remarkable how he got around on his one good leg and a crutch. He could climb stairs as fast as most men and could mount and ride a horse with ease. He was the jokester in the group of veterans and found humor in everything. Agnes always said she thought Walter used his laughter to hide some of the horrible things he endured in the war. Walter was always playing practical jokes on the other workers. As much as he talked and carried on with his friends he never mentioned his service in the war and how he lost his leg. In Walter`s mind it was if it had never happened.

OCTOBER 3RD 1862- 2ND BATTLE OF CORINTH-NORTHERN MISSISSIPPI
4TH INFANTRY REGIMENT- GENERAL VAN DORN`S ARMY OF WEST TENNESSEE

Private Walter Sloan marched with his company toward the center of Corinth.   The fighting had been heavy, but the advantage was on the side of the Confederates as the Union line moved farther back into the city.   General Van Dorn, sensing victory, halted the advance to allow his men to rest and receive much needed food and water. His plan was to attack in full force the following morning of the 4th.

General William S. Rosecrans, the Union commander at Corinth, took advantage of the break in the battle and shored up his defensive positions. He brought in three artillery batteries to repel the attack he knew would be coming the next day.

General Van Dorn planned to attack Corinth at dawn, but because of the sudden illness of General Louis Hebert, delayed the attack until nine o`clock. This mistake would give the Union artillery commanders a clear view of the attacking Confederate cavalry and infantry.

The attack was a disaster with over half of the corps falling in the first thirty minutes. Some of the Rebel units reached the city but not in enough numbers to be successful. Of the three companies of infantry to reach Corinth, all were either killed or taken prisoner.

Such was the fate of Private Walter Sloan. As Private Sloan crossed the fortification lines with his 6th Company of the Mississippi Rifles, he was shot in the ankle and slashed across the back with an officers saber. Walter Sloan fell unconscious to the ground, and didn`t know the outcome of the battle until he awoke in a Union aide tent inside Corinth.   He felt a stinging pain to his left leg. Upon inspection, he saw that the leg had been amputated just below the knee. He was told by the Union Surgeon that his lower leg was so mangled he had no course but to remove it. The doctor had also placed twenty two stitches in the young private`s back to close the gaping wound caused by the saber slash.

Walter was placed with about sixty other prisoners in a makeshift stockade hospital far north of the battle lines. He learned that General Van Dorn had retreated from the area and Corinth remained firmly in the hands of the Union Army.

Walter spent three months in the stockade hospital at Corinth. When the doctors were sure he could travel, he and five hundred other southern prisoners were sent to the new Union prison on the Delaware river simply named, Fort Delaware Prison. The journey to the prison was tortuous to all the men, but the numbing cold of late January was particularly painful to Water Sloan. His leg had healed properly but his back had festered and rarely left Private Sloan free of pain. The wagons were covered, but the one blanket provided by his captors did little to help.

The prison was made up of twenty five long buildings that had been quickly and poorly constructed. The buildings had holes and spaces in the floors that allowed the winds to pour in. A little heat was provided by an open pot bellied stove near the center of the building. On first arriving, the prisoners tried to work out a system where each man could spend at least two hours a day at the heater. As time went on the stronger of the men pushed forward and crowded out the weak. There was no chain of command as everyone in Walter Sloan's building were privates. The Yankee guards said the Rebel officers were kept in special quarters near the river.

At first the food was tolerable, but by the fall of '63 the men were almost starving. They were forced to catch mice and rats and all the crickets and roaches they could for food. Some days they were given two hard biscuits and some water. On other days it was a type of cornbread that the men said was only edible if it had weevils in it to add a little flavor. The men all suffered from dysentery, and by the winter of 1864 there were only 184 of the original 500 men still alive who had been brought from Corinth in the fall of '63.

Somehow Walter Sloan survived. A friendly guard made Walter a crutch from a tree branch. Walter became quite good at getting around on it. Walter was determined to live out the war. He was good with his hands and could fix anything about the pumps and other plumbing at the camp. The guards started bringing Walter an extra ration of food, and on a few occasions even let him have a real hen's egg and a piece of bacon.

When the war ended in 1865, Walter Sloan was released from prison and told he could go home. Walter had never been a large man, but when he was released he weighed just a little over 120 pounds. All he had was the clothes on his back and his crutch to get him to Iuka, Mississippi, some five hundred miles south.

The weather was nice in August in Delaware when Walter Sloan started his journey home. He got a ride as far as Charleston, South Carolina in a makeshift wagon with a peddler. Walter came upon the peddler one day, and the old salesman looked at Walter and said,

"Well, boy, from the looks of you they didn't feed you too good did they? Hop up in the wagon before you die right here on this old road."

Walter remembered the stories his preacher daddy had told back in Iuka when he was a young boy. One of his favorites was that of the Good Samaritan.   Walter knew that somehow his daddy's prayers had gotten up to God, and he had sent this kind peddler at just the right time to save Walter from dying.

It seemed every time Walter would get stranded, someone else would always come by and take him a little closer to home. He spent one night in Marietta, Georgia with an elderly couple who let him take one of their two horses. Walter told them of his trials, and they thought if this young Mississippi boy was that intent on getting home, they were going to help him.

Walter arrived in Iuka in November. He had been on the road for almost four months. He had not heard a word from his folks since he left home to join the Confederate Army back in 1862. When he went to the old home place his parents weren't there. The old house looked as if no one had lived there in some time.

Walter's daddy had been the Church of Christ preacher and had been highly respected in the small town. When Walter asked at the store on the square about his folks, he was told bad news. Both his daddy and mother had died during the Small Pox outbreak in '63. The lady at the store didn't know where Walter's sister, Frances was.

She hadn't been heard of in years. Everyone in Iuka thought Walter had been killed in the fighting at Corinth.

Walter Sloan had no money and no place to live. He found out at the court house his old house was not listed in anyone's name. It was assumed it still belonged to Walter's daddy. The house was in ill repair, but at least it had a roof on it. When Walter looked inside there was evidence some transients had used the home for shelter. There was still enough furniture to make a comfortable home. After what Walter had been through the past three years, the place looked like a palace.

Agnes Swanson, the owner of the stores on the square, and her daughter, Jenny Wade brought new sheets, towels and mens clothes to Walter. The women of the Church of Christ delivered several boxes of food to the house. Walter was humbled by the kindness of the wonderful people of Iuka. Agnes offered Walter a job at the stores and agreed to pay him twenty five dollars a week. Walter couldn't believe his good fortune. He threw himself into his work, and in just a few weeks became the chief handyman for all the stores. He was invaluable to Agnes and her family.

On Christmas Eve night when Walter arrived at his house, he found a package containing twenty ten dollar Eagles and a note that simply said,

"Thank you for your service to our country. You are an inspiration to us all. Please accept this gift as a token of our love and appreciation. Grateful friends."

Walter never knew who left the gold coins, but he knew the best way he could show his gratitude was to be the best citizen he could and help as many people as possible. He developed a wonderful sense of humor and brightened any gathering with his jokes and songs.

He gladly welcomed all the returning veterans hired by Agnes Swanson, and later by her grand son, Jedediah Wade. He would always speak to the new men and let them know how fortunate they were to work for such fine people.   He made sure no man ever faltered in his duties to his employers.

Walter knew his faith had helped keep him alive during his time at Ft. Delaware Prison. He wasted little time in becoming active in his daddy`s old church. By 1869, he was the song leader and director of all youth activities. The young people loved Walter and knew that Mr. Sloan was always available to council them in time of distress.

Chapter 19

The years from 1869 to 1890 were hard on a lot of the people, but you could tell that things were getting back to some form of normality. The southern states were again sending congressmen and senators to Washington. The state government was finally accomplishing some positive things. The legislature of the state put the schools back under state control. Teachers were being paid a livable wage to teach the young people of Mississippi.

The hurts and wounds of the mind had not healed for the people of the south, but with strong leadership and hard work, the towns and villages began to see good times again. Cotton reigned supreme, and Mississippi was still one of the top producers of the "White Gold" as cotton had been called in England.

We regularly got the Memphis Appeal newspaper and read with interest the articles about the cotton markets and the value of the Mississippi River in the handling of so much of the south's cotton crop.

Times were particularly good for the Wade families. Swanson's Stores continued to prosper, and Jed and Molly were fast becoming the business leaders of the city. Molly became a staunch worker for The Civil War Veteran's Relief Fund and spent many hours in speech making. On two occasions she traveled to the state capitol in Jackson to plead with the legislature to help destitute veterans and their families. Because of her efforts, veteran's homes were established in Holly Springs and Morton to house former soldiers who had no place to go. Most of the men who lived in the homes had been wounded in the war and could no longer make a living on their own.

On many occasions some of the veterans would receive bags of gold coins from some unknown benefactor to help ease their burdens. I never found out how Molly pulled this off but Jenny and I were extremely proud of her for her wise use of Mr. Lincoln's Gold.

We read with interest in the Appeal that the Federal Congress had allocated funds for the establishment of permanent Civil War Military Parks to honor the men on both sides who fought in the war. As I scanned the page, I saw that one of the battlefields selected was

Shiloh. I didn't know when, but I knew that some day I would have to return to that hallowed ground.

I stopped planting corn at the farm in `92. I was forty nine years old and my knees no longer held up to the plowing. I still kept a nice garden, and we had more than we needed. I had become a doting granddaddy and tried to see Jedediah and Laura Bell as often as I could.   The children liked staying out at the farm and playing with the animals. Charley, my faithful former Union Army horse, had long since passed away. We replaced Charley with a matched pair of brown geldings that were better suited to our larger wagon.   Jake, the Mule,was also gone but in his place we had a brand new mule named Bo that was even more gentle than Jake.   Bo would let the children sit on his back as I guided them around the yard.   Jenny welcomed a new stray dog into the family in 1889 and Rip was the king of the entire farm. He quickly took to Jedediah and Laura Bell. Whenever they were visiting he became their protector and made sure he was included in all activities.

On a beautiful fall day in October of 1893 Jed and Molly brought the kids out to the place for dinner after church. Agnes had been a little stove up with her lumbago but wanted us all to take a ride in the fresh air.   We decided to drive out to the cedar grove to check on the graves of the two young boys killed in the Battle of Iuka back in `62. Jed always liked looking at the graves of the people he was named for.   It was hard for Jedediah, Jr. and Laura Bell to understand about graves and death. They knew nothing of the war. We rarely spoke of it, and I am sure Jed and Molly never mentioned the war to them. The children had asked Walter Sloan what happened to his leg, and he always laughed and said, "a big old Yankee doctor chopped it off cause it had turned rotten." The children weren't really sure what a Yankee was.

That day at the cedar grove the children were very silent as they stood in awe looking at the crosses on the graves.   Jedediah was reading pretty well and could pick out the name on the young southerner's grave, "Jedediah Tomkins".

"He spelled his name just like I do," said young Jedediah.

Jed moved forward and gathered his two precious children to him and said,

"You and I were named for this young man, Jedediah. He was killed in the war along with the young northern boy in the other grave. His name was Albert, and we also have his name."

"Who killed the two boys, daddy?" asked Laura Bell.

You could see the anguish on her face as the innocent young girl couldn`t imagine someone killing another person.

"When you are a little older, we`ll explain it to you, honey. Right now help daddy clean the leaves off the boy`s graves, so they will look real nice."

Jed`s explanation seemed sufficient to Laura Bell as she lost herself in the task of picking up all the loose leaves from the graves. She seemed to have some inborn feeling about not stepping on the middle of the graves. I saw a tear in Jenny`s eyes as our precious grandchild carefully stepped around the mounds that covered the bodies of the two young boys. Jenny turned to me and with tears rolling down her cheeks whispered,

"They would be over fifty now, Marcus. Just wonder what they would have amounted to if they had lived."

Jenny`s words touched me deeply as my mind wandered back to that day in 1862 at Pittsburg Landing and seeing my best friend, Charley Rogers killed before my eyes. I thought of our good times together back in Galena. Charley was always an outgoing sort and I know had he lived he would be successful at whatever he had done. I hoped I would never forget Charley. He was the one good memory I had of my former childhood home.

APRIL 22, 1894–SHILOH MILITARY BATTLEFIELD
PITTSBURG LANDING, TENNESSEE

Sterling Ames stood at attention and saluted as he looked at the grave of Private Charley Rogers. The inscription on the small headstone simply said,

Private Charles A. Rogers
22nd Illinois Regulars

Former First Lieutenant Sterling Ames had come to the new military park at Shiloh at the request of his old commanding officer, Colonel Nathaniel Rogers. Colonel Rogers had asked Ames to tour the battlefield and find out anything he could about the 22nd Illinois Regulars and their exploits during the fierce battle back in April of 1862. Colonel Rogers had particularly asked Lieutenant Ames to find the grave of his nephew, Private Charley Rogers, and Charley's best friend, Private Marcus Wade.

Colonel Rogers had been devastated at the loss of his nephew in the first day of the battle. The Colonel never had a son and always thought of his sister's boy as his own. The Colonel knew that Charley and Marcus Wade had joined the regiment at his urging. He felt he had let them down by not protecting them better.

Back in 1862 Colonel Rogers had selected the western most encampment area at Pittsburg Landing and that decision was to cost him over half of his command in the first two hours of the battle. As the Confederate soldiers charged the Union lines, the first group to feel the brutal force of their onslaught was the 22nd Illinois.

Colonel Rogers had not seen Charley and Marcus fall, but he heard that Charley's body had been found the day after the battle ended. Marcus Wade's body was never found. It was assumed he was in such a sad state that what remained of his body was hastily buried in one of the large open pits surrounding the battlefield.

As former First Lieutenant Sterling Ames went from cross to cross in the beautiful cemetery overlooking the Tennessee River he tried to remember the faces of his men as he came upon each grave of a 22nd Regular soldier. The Park Commission had done a wonderful job in burying the boys from each unit next to each other. As Sterling Ames passed from grave to grave, he tried to recall something about each young man as he looked at their final resting place. He had only been twenty seven years old in 1862, and he knew that most of his command was made up of seventeen, eighteen and nineteen year old boys. He really liked Charley Rogers. He was a mild mannered, yet humorous sort and took his soldiering quite seriously. Had Private Rogers survived the battle at Shiloh, Lieutenant Ames was sure Charley would have made Sergeant in no time at all.

Charley's best friend, Marcus Wade, was a different breed, however. Sterling Ames had never liked Marcus. Ever since the first taste of battle at Fort Donelson, it was obvious that Private Wade had no stomach for fighting. He did his drills as ordered but showed no spark or spirit and seemed to have no desire for killing. At Shiloh, Lieutenant Ames knew that a large battle was imminent. He had made up his mind to thrust Private Wade into the center of any fighting when it broke out. He hoped that when Private Wade realized it was kill or be killed, he would become the soldier he was capable of being. Marcus was by far the best shot with a rifle in the brigade and could out march and out train any of his fellow soldiers. He just wasn't prepared to do what a good soldier had to do. Kill the enemy.

Lieutenant Ames silently walked around the hundreds of crosses in the huge cemetery and made his way over to the high bluff that sheltered Pittsburg Landing below. As he sat on a large stone and peered toward the calm waters of the Tennessee River moving slowly beneath him, it was hard for him to imagine the brutal battle that had occurred on this spot thirty two years before.

Sterling Ames remembered the morning of September the sixth, 1862 quite well. The men had just finished breakfast. He informed his company that they had forty five minutes to themselves before they would practice close order drill near the tent area. Some of the boys sat around the tents with their coffee and pipes. A few wandered off to inspect the surroundings. He remembered seeing Charley Rogers and Marcus Wade walk down to the small church building just up the main dirt road. Everything else happened so fast. In his mind the rest of that morning was just a blur. The Rebs had attacked in full force without warning, catching the 22nd Illinois totally by surprise. The men's rifles were still stacked outside the tents, and most if not all, were unloaded. Had Lieutenant Ames not herded his men toward the river they would have all fallen. Casualties were extremely high, but over half the regiment would regroup and fight again later in the day.

Lieutenant Ames and his men fought bravely on the 7th and regained all the ground lost on the 6th. They were a big part in the Union victory that sent the Rebel forces marching back toward Corinth. Sterling Ames didn't know until the morning of the 8th how many of his men were wounded, dead or missing. He was devastated when he got the final count.

Corporal Edmonds had found Charley Rogers' body and alerted Lieutenant Ames. When the Lieutenant saw Charley's condition, he knew he couldn't let Charley's uncle, Colonel Rogers, see his nephew's body. After two days of lying on the ground, Charley's body was frozen in a grotesque shape. The open wound in his head was full of ants and maggots. Lieutenant Ames ordered his men to wrap Charley in a blanket and bury him in the large trench that had been dug at the edge of the trees.

The Lieutenant found several more of his men who had perished that awful morning, but he never found the body of Private Marcus Wade. It was as if his body had been swallowed by the land. Word had come that some of the Union boys had been buried in another trench by Reb infantry. This wasn't uncommon during battles. Even though they were sworn enemies men on both sides respected the dead and treated them with dignity and honor.

When Lieutenant Ames returned to Cairo, Illinois, and reported to his old Colonel he told him how nice the cemetery looked back at Shiloh and how peaceful Charley's last resting place was.

The Lieutenant told Colonel Rogers that the Park Commission had done a remarkable job with the battlefield. He knew the old colonel would be happy to see the final abode of so many of the 22nd Illinois Regulars.

Lieutenant Ames reported that he never found any evidence of the presence of Private Marcus Wade's body at Shiloh Battlefield.

Chapter 20

We noticed Agnes having difficulty breathing just after Christmas of 1894. She had been coughing quite a bit, and the cold air of late December seemed to make things worse. Jenny and I knew Agnes was in distress and tried to make her as comfortable as possible. On Saturday morning December 30th, 1894 Agnes Swanson passed away. She was seventy two years old.

People from as far away as Birmingham, Alabama and Memphis, Tennessee came to Agnes' funeral. Seven of the veterans Agnes had employed at her stores served as her pall bearers. Former Captain Mark Lockhart was quite eloquent in his eulogy for "Miss Agnes."

"When I arrived in Iuka in '65, I was a broken man. I had lost all that was dear to me in the war. Miss Agnes Swanson gave me a job at her store and made me a welcome part of her extended family. In time, I found purpose to my life and enjoyed my twenty years here in Iuka and my employment at Swanson's. I can truthfully say that Miss Agnes Swanson was the kindest, most loving and generous woman I have ever met. She never turned a needy person away, and people would be amazed at the amount of money she handed out to strangers passing through. The lady was special in every way and will be sorely missed. It is doubtful that another like her will pass our way."

Mark turned to the family sitting on the first pew in the sanctuary of the Iuka Baptist Church and said,

"To you, Marcus and Jenny, and to you, Jed and Molly, I speak for all of the former soldiers here. We grieve with you in the loss of Miss Agnes, and pledge our undying support in the future. We will try to carry on in our work as she would have wanted us to. Miss Agnes once told me to always be kind to strangers as we will never know what problems they faced. This was the way she lived. We men here will try to follow her example. Because of her love for us most of the demons haunting us are long gone. I thank you for asking me to speak a few words about my adopted mother, Mrs. Agnes Swanson. May God give rest to her soul."

When Mark Lockhart sat down, you could hear the sobs throughout the church. Most in attendance knew of Mark`s exploits in battle and the tragedy that awaited him at home after the war when he discovered that his wife and children had been killed. The people knew that Mark`s words about Agnes had come from his heart.

Jed and Molly came out to the farm after the funeral. It seemed appropriate that a cold rain was falling. Our spirits had been dampened by the passing of Agnes and the rain just made things worse. Before the day was over the atmosphere at the farm lightened as we all shared special stories of Agnes.

We saw each other almost daily, but Jed was so busy with the stores that we really never had time to just sit and talk of life and precious memories. We grieved over our loss but knew the memories of Agnes would sustain us for years to come.

Jed said he wanted to know more of the war and what life was like around Iuka during the days of the fighting. He wanted to know all we could tell of Jedediah Tomkins and his family in Cherokee. He wanted to know what had happened at the store when the Yankees came and looted the entire town. I sat with Jed on the porch. My mind was filled with all the things Jed had been asking about. I leaned back in the rocker and the words simply flowed as I related story after story of the men we had met during the battle of Iuka. Jed sat spellbound as the past flashed before him. He knew some of the stories of the hardships suffered by the veterans working for us and knew how horrible the war had been. He never asked about the war again.

Chapter 21

After her mother died, Jenny seemed to lose all interest in the stores and was restless to travel. She had never been more than fifty miles from Iuka in her life. She urged me to consider a move to a larger city. We were now in our early fifties, and Jenny said she wanted to see more of the world while she was still young enough to enjoy it. Jed had a good grip on things at the stores and was more than content to live out his days as a merchant here in Iuka. Business had been quite good since the war. Jed had become a prosperous young man. Mr. Lincoln's Gold was there but Jed and Molly never used any of it for their own needs.

Jed and Molly made numerous good will trips to surrounding towns and hamlets and distributed hundreds of Mr. Lincoln's Gold coins to needy and deserving people. It had become Jed's passion in life, and Jenny and I were extremely proud of him.

We had, for some time been receiving the Memphis, Tennessee newspaper, The Memphis Appeal. Jenny was fascinated by the pictures of the Mississippi River and the large buildings of the city. Memphis was not quite a hundred miles away and I could think of no reasonable argument as to why we shouldn't at least look at the city as a second home. We could travel back and forth to see the children whenever we desired.

Jed and Molly didn't try to discourage us. They knew Jenny wanted this adventure in her life and were happy to support her in her decision to acquire a home in Memphis. We had checked property values in the paper and realized we could secure adequate accommodations in the range of five to eight thousand dollars. I felt it would only be right for Mr. Lincoln to foot the bill for this small extravagance in our lives.

It was decided. We made our plans, and on March 10th, 1895, we loaded the wagon and started for Tennessee. We decided to leave most of our furniture at the farm and take only those things we felt we couldn't get by without. Many years ago I had made a large storage shelf under the floor of the wagon. It was so well concealed it would be difficult for a passerby to notice that there were things hidden there. We carried fifteen thousand dollars of Mr. Lincoln's Gold with us. We felt this would be adequate for our needs. We had a bank account at the Iuka Bank with over ten thousand dollars on deposit. Funding our adventure should be no problem.

The heavily traveled road going west led us by Burnsville Store. We stopped and had dinner with Susan and Jubal Stokes at Eb Cayson's old place. Jubal and Susan had done wonders with the place. The peach trees were already showing signs of early blooms. It was easy to see that Jubal was where he wanted to be, and life had finally smiled with favor on him. We enjoyed our short stay with the Stokes but knew we had to get some miles behind us. I hoped to reach Memphis in four days, so we needed to cover at least twenty five miles each day.

On our second day on the journey, we stopped at a house just over the Tennessee line to ask if we could fill our water keg at their well. The couple appeared to be about our age, but the man was stooped and evidently not in good health. As we looked around, we could see that provisions were sparse in the home and there was no sign of livestock. The couple was very hospitable and urged us to rest awhile at their place. They even invited us to spend the night.

We introduced ourselves and found that Spence and Wanda Jenkins were natives of the area and that Spence had suffered badly during the war. His health had failed and he was unable to work the small farm. The Jenkins had a son who lived ten miles to the south. He came by as often as possible and tried to supply the couple with their needs. I could see Jenny was saddened by the meager surroundings.

Jenny told Wanda we had ample stores in our wagon and would love to share what we had for our supper together. It was obvious Wanda was slightly embarrassed by the suggestion, but their needs were such that she readily accepted Jenny's offer. Jenny went to our wagon and secured a slab of bacon, a bag of eggs and enough flour for biscuits.

As the four of us enjoyed our "breakfast supper" the couple shared their past with us. Spence told a harrowing tale of his experiences at Vicksburg during the war.

As we held each other in our arms in the nice spare bedroom at Spence and Wanda Jenkins home, Jenny and I realized how fortunate we were. The war had not scarred us as it had so many of the families in both the south and the north. Spence Jenkins was a perfect example of the total folly of war. The war had left him a broken man who had no future but to live out his days in pain and misery. The things he described about Vicksburg were so violent and cruel that it made my experience at Pittsburg Landing seem mild.

Before we went to sleep, Jenny and I agreed that Mr. Lincoln needed to take a part in the lives of Spence and Wanda Jenkins.

I slipped out of the bed and carefully made my way to the wagon. I counted out a thousand dollars in Gold Eagles, put them in a coffee bag, and placed them on the kitchen table. Jenny and I knew that in this instance it would be impossible for us to keep the family from knowing who gave them the money. Jenny wrote a note to Wanda and Spence and placed it on top of the bag of money. Just before sunrise we slipped out of the house and quietly moved down the road to Memphis.

Jenny's note was loving and to the point.

Dear Wanda and Spence,

We were so touched by your story and the unfortunate circumstances that have occurred in your life during and since the war. Marcus and I have been unusually blessed and want to share this gift with you. Maybe in some way it will help you to a happier life ahead. Thank you for your genuine hospitality. You are truly wonderful people.

Love,
Jenny Wade"

Wanda was the first to arise around six thirty and saw that Jenny and Marcus were gone. She first wondered if they had offended their guests in any way. She walked to the stove to make her morning coffee and noticed the bag on the kitchen table and the note from Jenny.

As she read the note and poured out the coins on the table, she bowed her head and sobbed. She whispered a prayer. "Oh thank you, Jesus. Thank you, thank you, thank you."

She walked to her bedroom door and waked Spence.

"Spence! Get up! You`ll never believe what has happened."

BATTLE OF VICKSBURG
MAY 13- JULY 4, 1863

President Lincoln informed his staff in early 1863 that the most important military objective in the war was Vicksburg, Mississippi. Vicksburg was situated on a high bluff overlooking the Mississippi River. Since the beginning of the war in 1861, traffic on the river had virtually stopped due to the artillery batteries commanded by southern forces. The battery commanders had a clear view of the boats on the river below. Not only had the north lost control of this vital artery of transportation, but the river provided the Confederates an unimpeded source of supplies from the south and west.

President Lincoln urged General Grant to take whatever steps available and move with haste on the "Gibralter of the Confederacy." General Grant devised a masterful plan of surrounding the city from the east while having Admiral David Porter form a virtual armada of gunboats below the city. After defeating the confederates at Raymond, Port Gibson and Champion Hill, Grant then captured Jackson, the capitol of the state. With no support from the east, Confederate commander of the Army of Vicksburg, General John C. Pemberton, ordered his entire force to form a defensive curtain from inside the city. It would be an unwise decision and eventually cause the destruction of Pemberton's grand army.

Corporal Spence Jenkins rode with his 43rd Tennessee Cavalry in the battle of Raymond. He and his fellow Rebels had fought bravely. Only the sheer superiority of numbers forced the 43rd to retire the battle. Spence Jenkins was slightly wounded in the left arm but never missed a day with his unit. The 43rd Tennessee was eventually ordered to Vicksburg to help in the defense of the city.

On May 13th General Grant ordered a concentrated attack on the entire line around Vicksburg. The fighting was intense all day. The Union army suffered staggering losses. The Confederate Army's location on the high ground and the emplacement of their heavy guns made the taking of Vicksburg by frontal assault impossible.

General Grant pulled his forces back and encircled the city, entrapping the entire thirty thousand Confederates with no hope of escape.

The bombardments started in earnest on the 20th of May. General Grant and his Army of the Tennessee fired their heavy weapons from the land, while Admiral Porter's gunboats rained heavy destruction from the river. Corporal Spence Jenkins and his cavalry unit became infantrymen and had to watch in horror as nearly all their trusted horses were killed by exploding Union shells. There was simply no place to hide the animals. Spence had always been a courageous man, but the constant pounding of the big guns and the explosions wore on his nerves. It was obvious after the 25th that no further land attacks were forthcoming. General Grant had decided to literally wait until all fresh water and food was gone in Vicksburg, and General Pemberton was forced to surrender.

Heavy casualties were suffered daily. The men dug holes under the embankments for protection but eventually the large Union guns would find their marks. The Rebel Artillery units did their part in returning fire and did heavy damage until all their ammunition was gone. On June 1st all remaining food was gone in the city. The civilian population gladly shared all they had, but trying to feed thirty thousand extra mouths was an impossibility. All remaining horses were killed and eaten by the troops. By late June, the men were trying to catch rats and mice to eat and were boiling dirt from smoke houses to gather some nourishment from the soil.

In desperation some of the men would try to raid Union encampments but were quickly killed or captured. There was little fresh water available as all the wells had been shattered by Union guns. A company of volunteers tried to steal away in the cover of darkness to contact General Johnston and advise him of the deplorable conditions in Vicksburg, but they were discovered less than two miles from the city and killed on the spot. There was no escape route out of Vicksburg in any direction.

Spence Jenkins first started coughing in mid June and by the 25th was spitting up blood. It was discovered by the three surgeons still alive in the city that typhus was rampant among the men. The men also suffered from dysentery and many had pneumonia. The overall condition of the Army of Vicksburg was deplorable, and on July 4th,

General Pemberton sent word to General Grant that he was ready to surrender the city.

When Grant's troops entered the city, the Confederate soldiers were given their first ration of food in over forty days. Most were too weak to eat.

After the siege of Vicksburg, some of the able bodied men were sent to Union prisons, but most were in such bad straits that General Grant told them to go home.

Spence Jenkins was near death and knew he would never make it the two hundred miles back to his home in Eastern Tennessee. He had left his wife, Wanda, and four year old son, Adam, to mind their small farm.

Spence and the most seriously ill Rebel soldiers lay near death in the Union hospital tent in Vicksburg. The decision was made by the Union doctors to send these men to the better equipped hospital in Jackson. Spence arrived at the main hospital in Jackson on July 20th and remained under the care of both Union and Confederate doctors for over three months. His breathing never returned to normal, and by the time the war was over in 1865 Spence Jenkins was still a very sick man.

Spence returned to his family after the war and lived out his days in virtual seclusion with his wife. Although not an official casualty of the war, Spence Jenkins' life as he had known it had been taken away by the horrors he experienced at Vicksburg.

Chapter 22

Jenny and I arrived in Memphis on March 15th, 1895. The city was enormous. As we moved our wagon into the downtown area, we were confronted by over a hundred carriages of various descriptions. Many were similar to our wagon with a make shift tarpaulin cover, but several were quite elegant affairs with two horses and three different seats to accommodate up to nine people. Jenny was particularly impressed by the well dressed ladies riding in some of the more elegant rigs. On one such contraption, we saw the driver stop at one of the many stores on Main Street and another helper disembark and help the ladies to the street. There had been some rain. The street was muddy so the young man simply lifted the young ladies up to the wooden walk in front of the stores. The ladies hats were huge and full of feathers. The only hat Jenny had ever worn was one to keep the sun off while helping in the field. I could see that she was smitten by the beautiful head pieces.

Stores of all types lined the street on both sides. We counted six saloons in a three block strip. We urged our horse to the top of a hill where we had an unobstructed view of the Mississippi River below us. The Tennessee had been quite large, but the giant river moving swiftly beneath us was overwhelming. I determined that there was enough water passing by each ten minutes to supply all the water needs in the entire country for a year. Strange boats with large wheels on the rear were tied up at the docks. One such boat pulled out into the river and the force of the large wheel turning rapidly moved the boat at a fast pace. I had seen one such boat back at Cairo in 1861 and recalled it been named a stern wheeler.

We were amazed at the sheer number of people in the city. It was a Friday afternoon and the weather was quite pleasant. The women must have been doing their weekly shopping as few men were seen. As we moved our wagon onto the road that ran parallel to the river, we could see numerous houses and businesses. Some appeared to be taverns. We soon came to a section that had signs outside advertising lodging and food. Jenny was tired so I stopped at a place that looked clean enough and enquired within about lodging for the night. The very courteous attendant at the desk said we could have a room for one night for two dollars or if we stayed a week it would be ten dollars for the week. When I found that my wagon and horse could be kept behind the building, I decided to take the room for one week. This would give us time to see some of the sights of the city, and also let us look for a home at our leisure.

I gave the attendant at the livery stable a dollar to keep an eye on my rig. He was quite pleased. I could tell he would be diligent in his job. He said he would unharness our horse and water and feed him.

Our accommodations in the inn were more than adequate to our needs. The bed was comfortable and the room had two chairs and a dresser. There was a single electric light hanging from the ceiling. It had a string hanging down that would turn the light on and off. Down the hall was a wash room and toilet. The building only had six bedrooms, so timing our visits to the toilet wasn't a problem. We never saw who did it, but each time we entered the toilet someone had emptied the waste from the stall and used some nice smelling oil to make the room feel fresh. Jenny seemed quite relaxed in our room. We had never stayed at a public inn before. Jenny couldn't believe that someone would come by and clean our room each morning. We had been on the road for several days and except the one night at Wanda and Spence Jenkins we had slept in our wagon. The warm water provided made for a refreshing bath. It was nice to finally wash off the grime from our journey.

There was a café next to our inn and the food was very tasty. The ladies who did the cooking were better than average at their trade, and we ate heartily at each meal. I thought the price of thirty cents per meal was a little much but I knew we were now in the city and should expect such extravagance.

After a nice first night's rest, we ate our breakfast and decided to stroll around the downtown area during our first full day in Memphis. Jenny reminded me of the ladies hats, and I knew I was in for some serious shopping.

We walked about two blocks from our inn to Main Street and started our exploration of the city. My shopping experiences had been confined to Swanson's in Iuka and an occasional trip to Mr. Shepherd's to buy a pig. I wasn't prepared for the different stores we encountered in Memphis. Many stores sold just shoes. Some only hats. There was even one store that sold only things made from leather. At Swanson's we sold all of those things in one building. The quantity and variety of merchandise was unbelievable. Jenny had always been rather talkative, but as we perused the different stores, she became very quiet as if in a dream. She simply couldn't take it all in.

Jenny saw several things she liked, but we made only one purchase our first day. Jenny couldn't find her parasol in the wagon when we entered the inn. She said she must have left it at Wanda Jenkins' house. The sky was quite clear but Jenny insisted she have a parasol to carry around with her. I didn't offer any complaint to her wishes and paid the nice young attendant $1.35 for a very pretty yellow parasol with a shiny black handle trimmed in silver. As we made our way down the street, it became quite clear to me why Jenny insisted on the parasol . Looking about I saw that every lady we met on the street was carrying her very special parasol. Even with no rain and little sun, a few of the ladies had their parasols open, gently twirling them in a slow circle as they walked. I made sure Jenny couldn't see the smile I couldn't keep off my face.

I could tell Jenny was spellbound by all the things about us. The sounds of the city were almost mystical. Piano's were playing from inside open doors of saloons. An occasional bell would peal from a distant church steeple. Laughing children could be heard from the second floor windows over the stores. Horses pulling the beautiful carriages had their special sounds as they trotted slowly up and down the street. Some were adorned with tinkling bells. We noticed an occasional public carriage passing by. We found that for ten cents you could get on and off anywhere on the route. We were having too much fun walking, but knew we would eventually have to try the public carriages.

I was overwhelmed by the smells. The constant droppings by the horses on the street was something I was very accustomed to. Having worked behind a plow for so many years, I knew this was a natural function over which the horse had no control. City workers with push carts could be seen on every block picking up the droppings almost as fast as they fell.

Sweet smells of open air flower shops were evident as was the smell of roasting peanuts from a vendor pulling his cart along the street. Most of the stores had their doors open. As we passed the stores we could smell the unmistakable aroma of freshly baked bread. Back at the Emporium in Iuka, Agnes had carried a few wax candles for sale. We passed a shop selling only lamps and candles of all descriptions. We wandered through the aisles of this unusual store and were rewarded by our decision with aromas so sweet and pungent we had no words to describe them.

In Iuka there were signs on all the buildings giving the name of the establishment but little else. Here on the streets of Memphis large brightly colored billboards advertised everything from clothing to carriages. Slogans such as, "Best Selection of Ladies Hats in the South." "Finest Hand Made Carriages in Memphis." "Ladies and Men's Shoes-All Sizes." "New York Style at Memphis Prices." "Clothing Made to Order- Just For You."

Jenny reached over and squeezed my hand as if to say. 'Thank you, and I love you.' Needless to say, we were both enthralled by the sights and sounds of Memphis.

We spent the entire morning strolling the streets and were a little tired. Jenny motioned to a shady park across the street with benches and a pretty fountain. We paid ten cents for a strange looking sandwich from a vendor at the entrance to the park. A large round sausage was enclosed in a roll. The vendor had put mustard and kraut on it. We bought a lemonade at a stand by the fountain and sat on one of the benches to enjoy our meal. The sausage sandwich with the kraut and mustard combination was delicious.

As we sat and rested squirrels and pigeons crowded around us looking for scraps from our meal. Jenny broke off small pieces from her roll and had quite a time feeding the animals.

We were talking about all we had seen when a nice lady came by and gave us a circular about a new Baptist Church that was now open for services on the north end of Main Street. Someone had drawn a crude map and it was easy to see where the church was. When I read the circular I drew back as the first word hit me like a bolt.

SHILOH BAPTIST CHURCH
234 NORTH MAIN STREET
MEMPHIS, TENNESSEE

Come and worship with us. Preaching each
Sunday at 10:30- Fellowship Dinner following.
Brother Matthew W. Swindle- Pastor

Livery available in rear. Expert attendants.

ALL FAITH`S WELCOME!

As I read the word, Shiloh I froze in time.   I could only think of
the first Shiloh Baptist Church I had seen back at Pittsburg Landing in
`62 and the horror of that day.   Jenny could tell I was shaken and
knew why. She pulled me close to her. We sat for a moment not
speaking.   Through all our years together we never spoke of the
battle. Jenny knew that the most terrible day of my life was not
something I wanted to talk about. As I sat in the arms of the person I
loved more than anything else in the world , I thought how my life
had changed that day. As terrible as the experience was, I knew that
had I not done what I did and left the battlefield I would never have
met Jenny and Agnes. I would probably be dead there at Shiloh or
some other battlefield site.   I thought of my best friend, Charley
Rogers and how quickly he died.   All of our marching and training
couldn`t help Charley when that cannon ball exploded and took off
the side of his head.   Different things went through my mind of all
the young men who had suffered so terribly in the war.   I thought of
Jedediah Tomkins, and the young Albert from Michigan, lying cold in
graves in the cedar grove outside Iuka, Mississippi. I thought of Mark
Lockhart and how he found his wife raped and murdered with her
children when he returned after the war. I thought of Jubal Stokes
and the shock he received when he found his family dead and his
property in Georgia sold for taxes. I thought of Walter Sloan who lost
his leg at Corinth and came home to find that all his folks had died of

disease during the war. I thought of Spence Jenkins and the agony he still went through each day because of his experiences at Vicksburg.

The war seemed a hundred years off, but when I looked at that fateful word "Shiloh" on the church circular, the terrible memories of those days returned.

I apologized for my rudeness to the lady who had given us the circular and thanked her for inviting us. I promised we would attend services as soon as possible.

Jenny and I finished our meal and looked at the beautiful flowers surrounding a large fountain. Gold fish of several colors were gliding back and forth, darting to grab crumbs of bread thrown in the pond by onlookers. The park was quite popular as people of all ages strolled the perfectly manicured lanes. I noticed a couple holding hands and surmised they were newlyweds. They just had that special look.

There were several monuments scattered throughout the park honoring Confederate Veterans of the war who had lived in Memphis. Their names and ranks were listed. There was a General Robert B. McKnight, who commanded the 8th Tennessee Infantry Division. I hadn't heard of General McKnight but I am sure he did his part in the war.

I knew Jenny and I would come again to this beautiful sanctuary nestled in the heart of the bustling city.

Chapter 23

We felt quite refreshed after our rest in the park. We resumed our exploration of the city. From the entrance to the park, we could see the top of a huge building to the east. We moved to a main intersection of Main and Union Avenue and turned left. Just before us was simply the most beautiful and elegant structure either of us had ever seen. At the top of the tall building was a huge sign; PEABODY HOTEL.

We went in the hotel through a strange glass door that turned as you entered and pushed forward. Several people could get inside the turning door at the same time, but it was necessary to keep moving or the door would sweep you forward. We spoke to a uniformed attendant at the entrance and found that the hotel had been open for about twenty years and had several hundred rooms for guests. I asked the elderly Negro man how much it cost to stay here and he said most rooms were five dollars a night but they had some rooms with large parlors that were ten dollars.

As Jenny and I walked around the spacious interior of the hotel and I gazed about, I knew

that in all my days to come I would never see a place as elegant as this. The inn where we were staying on Front Street was lit totally by single lights on a cord. This magnificent giant had huge hanging fixtures with bright light bulbs. All the stores we had gone in on Main Street had electric lights, but they were just single glass globes hanging from the ceiling. Here in the main room of the Peabody were four huge fixtures with at least forty lights in each hanging fixture. Jenny and I simply stood and stared upward for several minutes. It would be difficult for me to describe the rest of the adornment, but needless to say, someone with a lot of money had built this elegant structure.

We sat on a comfortable couch in front of a beautiful marble fountain. An attendant brought us a cup of hot tea. It reminded me of the sassafras tea Agnes had prepared during the war. I couldn't tell what spice was in it, but Jenny said she thought it was cinnamon.

We wandered about the spacious lobby of the hotel drinking in all the beauty and splendor, when we heard voices above us. There was a balcony that circled above the main floor and we could see men in Confederate uniforms leaving a large room and entering the hallway. Men were laughing, slapping each other on the back and obviously enjoying themselves.

"Look, Marcus," said Jenny. "Those are war veterans, and I bet they are having a reunion. Come on. Let's go up these steps and get a better look."

I urged Jenny to slow down as we climbed some marble stairs to the balcony. I saw a sign that said "Mezzanine". I figured the fancy word meant loft or balcony, but I wasn't sure.

Turning toward the crowd of gray clad men, we could see through the open doors of The Plantation Ball Room. We noticed a banner on the wall that said,;

30th REUNION- 42nd ALABAMA CAVALRY.
WELCOME - CONGRESSMAN FIGHTIN' JOE WHEELER.

We had heard many things about the famous Confederate General Joseph Wheeler through the years. He had been the youngest general during the Civil War on either side. As I recollect he was only twenty eight when he was made a Brigadier General. We knew nothing of his life after the war and didn't know he had been elected to the Congress of the United States.

As I looked at the men in the hall, I realized that they were all about my age. A few appeared to be a little older, but I estimated most were in their mid to late fifties. A few showed evidence of wounds from the war. Two men had missing arms, and one was on crutches supporting just one leg. I thought most of the men were quite spry for their ages. I caught myself in that thought and realized I had never thought of myself as getting old. I looked at my peers mingling before me and knew that age had slowly crept up us all.

In her usual outgoing way, Jenny spoke to several of the men and got a courteous response from them all. One thing I can say about southern men. They are quite genteel of manner and in every case, to my memory, treat ladies with dignity and honor. As I remembered my comrades in the Union Army, I can truthfully say the usual response by one of the boys in blue when seeing a lady would be some remark bordering on the vulgar.

As Jenny was talking to another of the veterans, we looked toward the ballroom and standing in the doorway was a tall figure of a man in the uniform of a Confederate General. This had to be the famous Fightin' Joe Wheeler. He was trim, yet not too thin in the face. As most of the men, he had a full beard and mustache. It is difficult to explain, but the man simply stood out in the crowd. He had a presence about him that commanded respect, and he was certainly getting it from his former comrades in arms. As the men passed by and shook the great General's hand, he acted as if each man was the most special person in the room. He had a kind remark for each of them. Although it would have surely seemed impossible after all these years, he called each one by his first name and rank. Surely some aide was prompting him. The sheer aura of the man was over-whelming. As I looked at General Wheeler, I knew that in my army we had no such person in command. I didn't even know him, but if he had come over to me and asked me to ride into battle with him today I would probably have done it.

Jenny was also smitten by the General. She watched as all the men passed by and without hesitation walked up to General Wheeler and stuck out her hand.

"General Wheeler, sir, I want to shake your hand and tell you how proud we are of you and let you know we appreciate what you did during the great war."

"Why, thank you, ma'am," responded the General in a way that made Jenny feel like the most important person in the room. "Is your husband among our group?"

"Oh, no." answered Jenny. "We were just looking around the hotel and saw the celebration up here. When we found out it was to honor you, we wanted to come and meet you and some of your men."

The General seemed sincerely impressed by Jenny's adoration and talked to her for at least three minutes before he was interrupted by another uniformed former officer. The officer told General Wheeler he was expected at the Mayor's office at four, and they needed to be moving on.

General Wheeler made the most of his exit from the group. It was clear if he were running for President everyone in the Peabody Hotel at that time would have voted for him.

After the General left, we wandered around in the large ballroom where the 42nd Alabama had just completed their two day reunion. On the wall were citations from General Robert E. Lee and Confederate President Jefferson Davis. One such citation mentioned the statement General Lee had issued during the war when he said that young Joe Wheeler was the finest Cavalry officer in the entire Confederate Army. When you consider the likes of Nathan Bedford Forrest and Jeb Stuart, this was a remarkable statement indeed. On a plaque hanging over the speakers stand several statistics about General Wheeler and the 42nd were listed. To me the most stunning were the five hundred skirmishes Fightin` Joe had participated in during the war. He had been wounded three times and had sixteen horses shot out from under him. Thirty four of his closest aides had been killed by his side throughout the war.

One plaque recognized the former General`s work in Congress and his efforts toward unification of the nation.

Jenny and I felt honored to have met the great man. In any army of any country in any war General Joseph Wheeler would have stood out. He had that kind of magnetism.

We saw two of the older veterans ease into a heavily padded double sofa and begin to chat. Jenny was standing behind the men. When she heard them speaking, she motioned to me. One of the men was doing most of the talking, and his subject was disturbing to Jenny. It seems the old gentleman had gone to quite a lot of trouble to get to the meeting and was telling his friend the details of his trials.

"Why, my laudanum has gone up to a dollar a bottle, and I can`t get through the day without it. They never did get that Yankee minnie ball out of my back, and it pains me terrible on most days."

As the two veterans continued to talk, it was clear the man doing most of the talking had not fared well since the war. His story told of untold pain and misery at home and the struggle he and his wife had experienced since the war just trying to exist on their small farm in central Tennessee. His wife had become a nurse for wealthy families in the region and by taking in washing and selling vegetables from her garden was able to keep food on the table. The old man had saved for over a year, so he could make this trip to Memphis for the reunion. His oldest son had sold a prize heifer for forty dollars and had given the money to his daddy.

"You know, Sam, if General Wheeler hadn't come by and scooped me up on his horse that day outside Chattanooga, I wouldn't be here now," said the old soldier. "He exposed himself to heavy fire by helping me, and I'll never forget it. I would have walked here to Memphis if I had to just to see old Joe Wheeler again."

The feeble veteran had a tear in his eyes as he slumped back in the seat and let out a long slow breath of air.

Jenny clasped my hand, and I could see she was crying. I knew before she spoke what she was going to say.

"We've got to help him, Marcus. You go get some of President Lincoln's Gold and give it to him this very day. I don't care how you do it, but you've got to think of something."

I certainly couldn't argue with my darling wife. If anyone deserved help, it was this old man sitting in pain on the Mezzanine Floor of the Peabody Hotel in Memphis, Tennessee.

I eased around in front of the two old veterans and could see the name tags on their lapels quite clearly. The old man who had done all the talking didn't notice when I jotted his name on a piece of hotel paper laying on a desk in the hall.

Sergeant Frank L. Stevens
42nd Alabama Cavalry
Brownsville, Tennessee

42ND ALABAMA CAVALRY- ARMY OF TENNESSEE CHICKAMAUGA CAMPAIGN- SEPTEMBER 23rd 1863

Sergeant Frank Stevens advanced forward with his squad of horse soldiers into blistering rifle fire from Union positions on a tree line bordering a sprawling Georgia farm complex. The men of the 42nd Alabama had been in numerous skirmishes against the Yankee army since joining General Joe Wheeler's Cavalry Corps in 1861.

119

Today's battle seemed more fierce as the constant rifle fire was taking it's deadly toll on men and animals. Sergeant Stevens ordered his men to pull up behind a rock fence north of the entrenched Union forces to wait further orders.   One of Sergeant Stevens' men brought him a rifle taken from a dead Yankee private at the base of the fence. On investigation of the weapon, Frank Stevens could see why his men were at a disadvantage in the fight.   On the chrome plate of the rifle were the words "Spencer Repeater."   As Sergeant Stevens further investigated the sleek gun, he saw that simply by lifting a lever up and down a new .52 caliber shell would slip into the chamber allowing the shooter the luxury of firing seven shots without reloading.

Since the fall of `62 General Wheeler's Corp had been issued Sharps' rifles.   These bolt action, single shot weapons were quite efficient and were far superior to the muzzle loaders the troops had fought with in 1861.   The gun the Union soldiers were using here, however, changed tactics tremendously, as it would be suicide to ride directly into a line of men firing repeating rifles.

Sergeant Stevens sent a rider to the rear with the weapon to show to General Wheeler. Joe Wheeler had heard of the new gun but had never seen one. His reaction was fast and decisive. He sent word to his commander, General Braxton Bragg, to order an immediate artillery attack on the woods where the Union forces were entrenched. He told his Brigade commanders to wait until the end of the artillery barrage and attack the woods from three sides.

The plan worked perfectly as the Confederate Cavalry struck the Union lines before they could recover from the severe cannon fire. The Union line broke and the men not killed or captured moved quickly to the rear.

The battle continued throughout the day, but the action of Fightin' Joe Wheeler and his 42nd Alabama had turned the tide in favor of the Rebel forces.   Union General William S. Rosecrans, commander of the Army of the Cumberland, had his men retire the field of battle and move north toward Chattanooga.

Sergeant Frank Stevens lost six good men in the fight, but he was proud of his boys and the job they did that day. Sergeant Stevens watched in awe each time his commander, General Wheeler, made a correct decision on the battle field. The young general was always at the front of the fight, and many times led some of the fierce charges of his well mounted cavalry troops. On more than one occasion Frank had seen General Wheeler's horse shot from under him. The General had been slightly shaken but always got up, brushed himself off and remounted another horse to continue to lead his men.

On the day after the battle at Chickamauga, General Wheeler himself rode up to Sergeant Stevens' encampment behind the Georgia farm house and told the men that General Bragg had ordered the 42nd to pursue the Yankees and try to keep them from getting to Chattanooga. Frank Stevens had met General Wheeler on several occasions. The two young men, both age twenty eight, were more than speaking acquaintances. General Wheeler had recognized the expert horsemanship exhibited by then Private Frank Stevens in actions throughout the Tennessee Valley and had made Frank a Sergeant and put him in charge of a squad of horse soldiers.

The men were allowed to rest their animals throughout the day and night and eat a hot meal of boiled corn taken from the fields the day before. One of Frank's men shot a racoon from a tree limb and the squad enjoyed fresh meat with their corn.

General Bragg sent supply wagons to the front lines and the men stocked up on ammunition, food and water before advancing toward Chattanooga on the 25th.

The Yankee's anticipated the Confederate's move and virtually destroyed all the farms and crops from Georgia to Chattanooga. All bridges were blown, and the action caused some distress to General Wheeler. On the 29th of September, the 42nd caught up to stragglers of the Army of the Cumberland and caused them to scatter, leaving equipment of all description on the field for the taking. Several of the new Spencer rifles were confiscated, and General Wheeler assigned them to his best marksmen. He immediately moved them to the front of the attack.

Just outside of Chattanooga, General George H. Thomas, second in command of the Union forces, ordered his two brigades to form a defensive position using the natural hills surrounding the city as cover. The tactic was brilliant and allowed the rest of Rosecran's Army of the Cumberland to enter the city and firmly secure it.

General Wheeler had anticipated the move by the Union forces and led his men to the right flank in the hopes of entering the city from the east. Union pickets mounted atop high mountains could see the movement of the Rebel cavalry. They sent word to General Rosecrans inside the city. By the time the 42nd Alabama reached General Wheeler's desired location, the Union artillery batteries were already in position, supported by a full brigade of infantry.

The 42nd made one brave charge against the heavily fortified Union lines but were repulsed at every position. Sergeant Frank Stevens' men were assigned the area closest to General Wheeler. It was evident to Sergeant Stevens and all the officers that their position was futile, and the advantage was on the side of the much larger Union force.

General Wheeler realized his situation was impossible and sent word for his men to move east and regroup to fight again another day. Just as the order was given, a huge volley of rifle fire was thrown at the 42nd from Union infantry situated on high ground not two hundred yards to the west. Several men in gray fell instantly. Sergeant Frank Stevens was struck in the back by a shot from one of the Spencer rifles. Frank fell to the ground in severe pain and watched as his faithful horse, Windsong, fell by him. General Wheeler saw the action and instinctively galloped to the aide of his fallen sergeant.

"Quickly, Frank!" shouted the General. "Take my hand."

In one fast move General Wheeler leaned from his saddle and took the hand of Sergeant Stevens, pulling the man up behind him on his own horse. General Wheeler swiftly led his remaining men to the rear. There the General eased Sergeant Frank Stevens to the waiting arms of some of the aides at the Surgeons wagon.

"Good luck, Frank," said Joe Wheeler. "Get well soon. I need men like you to finish this war."

"Thank you, General, I'll do my best," said Frank Stevens through the worst pain he had ever felt.

The Union forces made no attempt to follow General Wheeler and the 42nd Alabama. The men of the north were exhausted from their battles in Georgia and were perfectly content to settle down behind secure fortifications in Chattanooga.

The Corp Surgeons set up tents near the Carolina state lines to tend to the wounded from Chattanooga. Sergeant Frank Stevens was one of the first to receive treatment as he had lost considerable blood. He was almost dead by the time the surgeons operated on him. Colonel Wilson, the Chief Surgeon in the 42nd Alabama, operated on

Frank.   When he saw the position of the bullet lodged next to the spine and between two main arteries, he knew he would kill Sergeant Stevens if he tried to remove the bullet. He closed the wound and told his aides to provide the sergeant with all the Laudanum he wanted when he awoke. The Colonel said that Sergeant Stevens would be in severe pain and would need the opiate to ease him as much as possible.

Sergeant Stevens was carried to the Confederate hospital in Charleston, and although near death for several months, survived. He spent the last year and a half of the war on the grounds of the hospital. He had become dependent on the Laudanum and couldn't make it through a day without at least a third of a bottle. When the war ended, Sergeant Stevens was told to go home.   He secured transportation on a train to Memphis and on August 18th, 1865 arrived at his home in Brownsville, Tennessee.

Frank Stevens could walk but could do little else.   His wife lovingly tended his every need. She worked at odd jobs around the town to provide for the family.   The Stevens had one son who did what he could to help his mother and dad.

Throughout the years   Sergeant Frank Stevens received regular letters from General Joe Wheeler. Frank Stevens knew he owed his life to his former commander and was thankful to have known and served with the great General.

In one of General Wheeler's letters a bright blue and gold medal was enclosed. Included was a printed citation that read;

"To Sergeant Frank Stevens of the 42nd Alabama Cavalry. For outstanding leadership and exemplary devotion to his commander and his country, I am proud to present to Sergeant Frank Stevens the Confederate Order of Merit. On many occasions Sergeant Stevens exposed himself to deadly fire and continued to lead his men without a thought of retreat.   Few men served their nation as well as Frank Stevens.

I am honored to sign this proclamation and to present it to one of my most faithful soldiers and my dear friend.
General Joseph Wheeler
Commanding Officer, 42nd Alabama Cavalry."

At the bottom of the letter General Wheeler had written Frank a personal note in his own hand,

"Sorry, we were so long in getting this to you, Frank. Hope to see you some day. Joe Wheeler."

In later years, Frank received word that General Wheeler had been elected to the congress of the United States of America. Frank wasn`t surprised.

Chapter 24

Jenny and I went down the stairs from the Mezzanine and walked over to a beautiful walnut counter where two young men in coats and bow ties were on duty as desk clerks. I asked if the men could tell me what room Mr. Frank Stevens was in. The smaller of the two young men turned to a large book and told me he was in room 436. Jenny asked the desk clerk if he knew when Mr. Stevens would be checking out. The young man looked at the book and said Sergeant Stevens was due to leave tomorrow morning.

Jenny and I walked back to The River View Inn on Front Street. I went to the livery stable to get the money from the wagon. We had decided that the hiding place under the seat was more secure than any other place we could have hid the gold. I spoke to the attendant and informed him I wanted to check on the horse and make sure there was plenty of grease in the wheels. Although this was an outright lie, I had heard some sounds from the left rear wheel. I went through the motions of looking at it.

The attendant was called away by another customer, and I was free to remove the cover of the hidden chest under the floor of the wagon without detection. Jenny and I decided to give Mr. Stevens one thousand dollars. I removed one hundred of the Gold Eagles and placed them in a sturdy bag Jenny had made. Although there was considerable weight to the coins, I was able to secure them inside my coat without much discomfort.

Jenny and I talked at length about how we would get the money to Sergeant Stevens. We finally decided that to make sure he got the coins and could protect them in his own way, we would have to present them to him in person. We were dressed quite nicely, and to any observer we could pass as wealthy cotton merchants or land owners. Gold coins were in regular use in 1895, and no one would ever associate our gift with President Lincoln and his missing gold. We simply decided that Jenny would tell the truth to Frank Stevens. We would let him know we had overheard his story at the hotel and wanted to present him this gift of love and appreciation.

We decided to wait until the next morning, so Frank Stevens wouldn't have to worry about someone stealing his gold during the night.

Jenny was quite excited and rose earlier than usual. We were in the café next door to the Inn at six o'clock enjoying a hearty breakfast of eggs and bacon. Jenny was afraid Frank Stevens would rise early himself and leave the hotel before we could give him the gold.

It took us less than ten minutes to walk to the Peabody. We were standing in the lobby by seven o'clock. There were a few men sitting around reading the newspaper, but otherwise there was very little activity that early in the morning. Jenny recognized two of the men as veterans she had spoken to the day before. The men had put away their Confederate uniforms and were neatly dressed in coats and well pressed trousers.

We made our way to the fourth floor and knocked on the door of room 436. We could hear movement inside, and knew that Mr. Stevens was up and about. Frank Stevens opened the door and was fully dressed. He had his bag on the floor by the door. We hadn't come a minute too soon. Jenny was first to speak.

"Mr. Stevens, I am Jenny Wade and this is my husband, Marcus. We wonder if we could have a word with you."

Frank Stevens had evidently had his morning dose of Laudanum as he was in relatively good condition. It was obvious that any movement caused him pain but he was very alert and courteous in his response.

"Why, certainly ma'am. Come right in. What can I do for you?"

I let Jenny do all the talking. She explained to the old sergeant how we overheard his conversation with his friend on the previous day, and we knew his distress and also his condition at home. Jenny was very polite in telling the old veteran how we would like to help his family's strained condition by giving him some money. Jenny let the old man know how much we appreciated his sacrifices during and after the war, and since we had been so overly blessed we wanted to share our good fortune with him.

Frank Stevens never said a word as Jenny spoke. He wasn't quite sure what he was hearing and didn't know how to react. Only when I handed him the heavy sack of coins did he show any emotion. As he opened the draw string on the bag and poured the coins on the bed, large tears began falling from his eyes. Without shame he lifted his head and spoke slowly and with difficulty.

"But why would you do this? I didn`t do anything that thousands of other boys did, and they didn`t make it home. I, at least am alive and have a wonderful wife and a comfortable place to live."

He couldn`t continue and Jenny walked to him and put her arm around his shoulder.

"You and your wife have suffered terribly, Mr. Stevens. Maybe this will ease your burden somewhat."

Frank Stevens knew he and his wife`s lives would be drastically changed by this gift of a thousand dollars. He could purchase seed corn for his son and buy his wife a new dress. He could buy the paint for the front of the house. He could have the barn door put back up. He didn`t know who these people were that had knocked on his door, but he knew they had been sent from God. He could tell from the attitude of the couple the money was given in the spirit of love and not pity. He gathered his emotions and said, "You will never know how much I appreciate this. I must admit that we need it badly. I have been concerned for my wife`s health and now she will be able to slow down a bit. I thank you with all my heart."

Frank Stevens and I discussed the money and the best way to hide it. Frank said he would put it in his bag and secure a little rope to the bag and to his wrist. He smiled, and said he didn`t intend to let the bag out of his grip until he arrived back home.

Sergeant Frank Stevens shook my hand, and he and Jenny embraced. It was a good feeling. We stayed in the lobby until we saw Mr. Stevens check out of the hotel and get in a carriage out front with one of his friends. He told us his friend was going to drop him off at Brownsville late this afternoon.

As the wagon pulled away and moved east on Union Avenue, Frank Stevens turned and smiled at us. Jenny reached over and squeezed my hand tightly. I looked at her, and as the morning light hit her face, she really did look like an angel.

As we walked back up Union Avenue, the activity on the streets had picked up considerably. Carriages were moving steadily about and store owners were opening their shops. Jenny motioned to a man opening the door to a real estate business we had passed the day before. We decided to inquire inside about the availability of housing in the city.

We gave the rotund man time to turn his overhead light on and place a few things on his desk when we entered. Jenny looked up at the sound of a tinkling bell that rang when the door opened. Jenny recognized it as one very similar to the bell Agnes had installed back at Swanson's in Iuka. It quickly let the proprietor know when a customer entered the door.

"Well, come in folks," said the portly man. He had taken off his hat, and we could see the only hair on his head was just over his ears. "What can I do for you this bright September morning?"

He reminded me of Sam, one of the drummers who called on Agnes for years. Sam was eternally cheerful and used his personality as a selling tool.

I stuck out my hand and introduced myself and Jenny. His name was Mr. Porter. I informed Mr. Porter that we had just arrived in Memphis and would like to purchase a house as near town as possible.

You would have thought we were the King and Queen of England by his response. He quickly moved to a group of large sheets hanging on the north wall of the room and said,

"Mr. Wade, you are in luck. I have two very nice properties available. One is just north of downtown and the other one block below the train station on the south end. Let me show you these drawings of the places."

Jenny and I moved to the wall and could see several drawings of commercial buildings and vacant lots. Mr. Porter finally got to the pictures he wanted and pulled them from the group.

We looked at both drawings but could tell very little about the actual houses from the pictures. Mr. Porter could see our problem and suggested we get in his carriage and investigate each of the places in person. The owner of Porter Real Estate said his wife was next door chatting with the ladies in the dress shop, and she could come over and keep the office while we looked at the houses. We met Mrs. Porter and started our journey to look for our new home.

It took about two hours for us to see both places. We both liked the house below the train station best, but Jenny said she didn't like all the traffic and noise around the depot. The house just off north

Main Street was smaller but adequate to our needs. The neighborhood was quiet and peaceful. There was a shed out back large enough for our wagon and a nice stall for our horse. Mr. Porter pointed out a small grocery store on the corner down the street, and I smiled when I saw the Shiloh Baptist Church sign less than two hundred yards north.

We found that the previous owners had moved to Pittsburg, Pennsylvania to be with ailing family. They had told Mr. Porter to get what he could for the place. We were prepared to pay up to seven thousand, if necessary, but were very pleased when Mr. Porter offered us the house, barn, storage building and lot for forty two hundred dollars.

Jenny investigated the house's interior carefully and determined that the previous owners were well bred people as the house was in wonderful condition. The owners had also left some nice sheer curtains on the front windows. The house had a living room, parlor, dining room and two bed rooms. There was indoor plumbing in the kitchen and bathrooms and Jenny was thrilled with the electric lights hanging from the ceilings in each room. We had never had electricity at home in Iuka. This was a nice surprise for us.

We agreed to purchase the house and made our plans to move in. Mr. Porter pointed out two nice furniture stores on Main Street. We filled all our needs for less than four hundred dollars. Jenny didn't put any furniture in the second bedroom as we had no use for it unless Jed and Molly and the kids visited us.

We moved into our new home on October 1st, 1895. We joined the Shiloh Baptist Church the following Sunday. Jenny made friends with Stella Wadkins, our next door neighbor, and I could see a side of Jenny I had never seen. Jenny was starved for the company of another woman. Ever since Agnes died, Jenny and I were together by ourselves at the farm and rarely saw other people. Jenny and Stella talked each day for hours and shared cooking ideas and fashion news. I knew I needed to give Jenny and Stella their time together.

The river was magical. We could walk one block from our house and have a perfect view of The Mississippi River and the activity at the docks. We spent many hours at the river front watching the loading and unloading of cotton and other goods. Jenny loved to talk to all the people getting off the boats. Many were from as far away as Michigan and Ohio.

I met Simon, a jolly fisherman, who supplied us with fresh fish at least twice weekly.

Life in Memphis was totally different than Iuka. We loved Iuka and it's closeness, but Memphis provided things we had never seen or experienced. Jenny loved her new home, new friends, the church and the city. There was something about Memphis that captivated Jenny, and I knew she was happier than she had been in years.

I had begun taking daily walks and met several men on my journeys. The men my age had all fought with the south in the war. Curtis Monts, a writer for the Memphis Appeal, lost an eye while fighting with Beauregard in northern Louisiana. Jack Reed rode with Forrest and actually fought a battle right here in Memphis. He liked the people of Memphis and their hospitality to him and moved to Memphis in `66, married a local girl and opened a men's haberdashery just off main street. I think the man who impressed me most was Woodson Clark. Woodson was the proprietor of the corner grocery store where Jenny and I bought all our food needs. Woodson was totally bald, yet trim and fit. I assume he was around fifty five or six since he told me he joined the Confederate Army in `61 when the war started. Woodson was normally very happy and always had a joke for his customers. Jenny loved to shop at Clark's Grocery, and one of the main reasons was Woodson himself. Woodson became a dear friend. At times I would rise early and stroll down to Clark's just as Woodson was opening the store. He would have a pot of coffee on the pot belly stove, and on more than one occasion we would sit and talk for quite a spell about everything from politics to the new gas powered automobile. The Appeal had run a story that in Europe some one had invented an engine that would run a carriage by using gasoline as fuel.

One morning while we were talking, it started raining, and I saw Woodson gaze out the front of the store. I noticed Woodson's countenance change. His face lost the grin that was always present, and it was obvious his mind was in another place. We had talked little of the war, and I only knew that Woodson had been a corporal with the 34th Tennessee Volunteers and had fought with General John Bell Hood's Army of Tennessee in battles throughout the state.

Woodson told me of battles and experiences too bitter for any man to forget. When I left the store that morning, I had a new respect for my new friend and thought of the old adage Agnes had used many times,

"You wouldn't knock on a neighbor's door and ask to swap troubles with anyone."

How right my former mother in law was. All the men I had met in Memphis had their own stories and each had his own ghosts from the past.

It just seemed to me that Woodson Clark's story of his experiences in the war were special.

He had suffered greatly, and the memories of those days were still fresh in his mind.

NOVEMBER 24-30, 1864 - FRANKLIN-NASHVILLE CAMPAIGN
GENERAL JOHN BELL HOOD`S ARMY OF TENNESSEE

Corporal Woodson Clark marched with the 34th Tennessee Infantry as they crossed the Alabama-Tennessee line at Florence with General John Bell Hood`s Army of Tennessee. General Hood had assembled a potent fighting force including infantry, cavalry and artillery. Leading his Cavalry Corps was the brilliant General Nathan Bedford Forrest. Hood`s aim was to sweep the Union Army out of Tennessee, set up a command post at Nashville and then consolidate even heavier forces to drive General William T. Sherman out of Georgia.

General Hood met resistance from General John M. Schofield`s 4[th] Army Corps just outside Columbia, Tennessee on November 24th. Hood had planned to cross the Duck river upstream from Columbia and cut the Union army`s line of communications with Nashville. General Schofield and his men left Pulaski and arrived in Columbia just in advance of Hood`s forces. Hood advanced his infantry on the following day but due to foul weather did not attack. Realizing his disadvantaged position, General Schofield retired his entire Union corps and moved toward Spring Hill on the 28th.

Corporal Woodson Clark and his squad of regulars were sent ahead with three company`s of the 34[th] Tennessee to support General Nathan Bedford Forrest`s Cavalry in their attack on stragglers of Schofields Union Army of the Cumberland. One brigade of Union infantry had fallen back and formed a defensive position in a stand of trees lining the main road from Columbia to Spring Hill. The Yankee brigade let General Forrest`s cavalry pass by without giving away their position. As Corporal Clark and his men moved north, they were suddenly met with blistering rifle fire from the Union lines behind the trees. Woodson Clark felt a sharp pain on his forehead as his hat was blown off. A shot from a Spencer repeating rifle had grazed his head but did little damage. As Corporal Clark tried to get his men to safe ground he saw six of his boys fall. Lieutenant

Stallings told the men to get in the ditch by the road. In less than five minutes over one hundred of the three hundred southern boys fell to their deaths on the Columbia-Spring Hill road. The position of the Yankees was on high ground and the trees provided enough cover to prevent much damage from Rebel guns.

Corporal Clark knew the only hope he and his men had was for help to come from another quarter. It came from the north as two company's of General Forrest's Cavalry quickly rode onto the scene and drove directly into the woods on top of the entrenched Union infantry. The Yankee boys were no match for the experienced horsemen and quickly left their positions and started running away from the battle. The skirmish was over in ten minutes.

Corporal Woodson Clark shook the hand of one of the riders as the cavalry came to offer assistance to the wounded men on the road. The rider told Woodson that some of General Forrest's rear guard heard the rifle fire, and the General had sent his men to assist his fellow soldiers. Corporal Clark told the young rider if they had been ten minutes later none of the infantry would have been left to shake his hand.

There was sporadic action in Spring Hill, but Schofield's main force had moved on to Franklin. Franklin had been in Union hands since Nashville fell in '63. Not known to the Confederate leaders, Franklin had been heavily fortified and sturdy wooden emplacements had been built to repulse the heaviest of attacks. General Schofield had his men take a defensive position behind the fortifications, forming a semicircle around the southeastern part of the town. The heavily entrenched Union forces were stretched out for over two miles making entrance into Franklin virtually impossible.

General Forrest reported back to his commander, General Hood, that his investigation of the area showed any attack directly on Franklin would cause the loss of many good men and had little hope of success. General Hood had been trailing Schofield for four days, and he felt his only chance of keeping the Union General from reaching Nashville would be to stop him here at Franklin. General Hood made a fateful decision. He gathered his entire corps together and ordered his twelve subordinate generals to lead their men on a direct assault of Franklin.

The attacks started at 4:00 in the afternoon of November 30. Corporal Woodson Clark and the 34th Tennessee was assigned to General Otho Strahl at the right center of the town. The first attack was by the cavalry and Woodson watched as more than four hundred brave riders fell in the first assault from heavy rifle fire and artillery bursts. He saw two Cavalry Generals shot from their horses in the first wave against heavily fortified Union positions. Only a handful of men and even fewer horses made it back to the Confederate lines. Corporate Clark was in awe at the bravery of the horsemen in gray as they rushed into certain death.

General Strahl moved to the front of his infantry corps and with his saber held high urged his full brigade of infantry forward. Woodson Clark was no more than twenty feet away when he saw the General stagger and fall with two bullet wounds to the chest. Men were dropping all around Corporal Clark, but the gray line continued moving forward. At one point, two company's broke the Union line and caused heavy casualties to the men in blue. The small victory was short lived as Yankee reinforcements from the center of town moved forward to drive the Rebs back through the lines.

Corporal Clark evaded capture by grabbing the neck of a galloping Rebel cavalry horse that had lost it's rider. The horse was trying to free himself of the carnage and return to a friendlier position. Woodson fell from the horse after hanging on for over fifty yards. When he scrambled to his feet, he joined three other gray clad boys to his left, all moving as fast as they could to the rear.

The first attack was a total disaster. Casualties were too high to count. Heavy Confederate casualties were reported from every position, but General Hood again ordered his men to regroup and attack.

In all his other battles Woodson Clark had seen commanders on both sides pull their men back at sundown and wait until daylight the next day to continue the fight. This was not the case at Franklin. Well after dark General Hood kept giving the same order, "Attack."

The fighting continued until nine o'clock before the sounds of battle ceased. Early morning, December 1st, General Hood ordered his men to retire the field. His broken, weary Army of Tennessee moved toward Nashville leaving Schofield and his Union Army virtually intact in Franklin. The cost had been enormous. Over six thousand Confederate soldiers were killed in five hours. An unprecedented six Generals were among the dead. The Union forces lost over two thousand men making Franklin, Tennessee the bloodiest five hours of the war.

As Corporal Woodson Clark marched with his remaining men toward Nashville, he was a broken man. He had bravely fought in over thirty battles for his country, but the hell of the day had taken his spirit. He had always respected the chain of command and had followed every order given, but what he had witnessed this day was not only a mistake but blatant stupidity.

General John B. Hood would suffer another defeat at Nashville. What was left of his once mighty Army of Tennessee fled south and crossed the Tennessee River. When Hood arrived in Tupelo, Mississippi he resigned his command. The once proud General and leader of men was considered a failure by his fellow southerners. General Forrest and others who served with Hood considered the decisions made at Franklin to be the worst by any General during the war. They never forgave their former commander.

Corporal Woodson Clark would be wounded twice before the war ended, but survived and returned to Memphis in 1865. He took three hundred dollars his father had left him and opened a small grocery store on the north end of town. He married his sister's best friend, and they had three girls. One of his wounds had been to his right buttock. Woodson made a reputation for himself telling funny stories about this unusual wound. Men who knew him and those who served with him, however, told stories of unusual bravery and devotion to country. He was considered a hero to all who really knew him.

Chapter 25

Jenny wrote the kids regularly and told them we were going to visit Iuka for Christmas. We found for three dollars and fifty cents each we could ride the train from Memphis to Corinth.

Jed met us at Corinth in the wagon. The ride to the farm was very pleasant. It gave Jed time to catch us up on all the happenings around Iuka. We loved seeing all our family. We brought several presents to Jedediah, Jr. and Laura Bell and enjoyed the looks on their faces as they opened the packages.

Jed had a great selling season the fall of 1895 and decided to open a division of Swanson's in Tishomingo, a small town south of Iuka. Jed made a few travels with Sam, the drummer from Birmingham, and they both decided that Tishomingo needed a store like Swanson's.

Jenny and I returned to Memphis on January 10th with a good feeling in our hearts. Our son and daughter- in- law were doing a great job of raising our grandchildren and we were happy in Memphis.

In the spring of 1896, Jenny and I decided to take a river cruise to New Orleans. We had inquired at the docks on the river and found that the River Queen made regular trips down the Mississippi. For forty four dollars each we could travel in style for two weeks.

We boarded the River Queen on April 23rd and were placed in a stateroom on the starboard side of the boat. The room was small but very nice. We weren't pleased with the two small beds on each wall, as we had never slept apart in all our married years. Jenny laughed and said I would have to crowd in her bed occasionally to keep her feet warm. Even at fifty six Jenny still had her coy ways of letting me know her bed was always open to me. As I looked at Jenny removing her hat and putting her things away, I realized how much I loved this pretty southern girl. Each night when I said my prayers, I thanked God for sending me into Swanson's that day back in 1861, when I met Jenny and her mother.

The river boat was huge. I walked from the stern to the bow and counted a hundred and forty two steps. I knew my stride was about three feet, so I estimated the total length of this massive boat was over 420 feet long. There were four decks above water. The first deck housed the dining area, bar, card room and reading room as well as the kitchen and food storage. The top three decks were staterooms. The captain told us the boat could carry up to two hundred passengers and crew.

We were allowed to go anywhere we wanted on the boat. When I went below deck, I was amazed at the horses and other livestock being transported. A huge area for cargo was in front of the animals, and hundreds of bales of cotton and finished goods were packed tightly together.

The engine room was not as large as I had assumed but was an amazing assortment of valves, pipes and huge ovens. Muscular men shoveled wood into the ovens and the heat was quite intense as the fires inside formed a virtual inferno. I was told by one of the workers the fires produced steam that went through the pipes and provided the force to turn the huge paddle wheels at the rear of the boat.

The scenery along the river was breathtaking. Many native flowers and trees were in full bloom and the temperature was very pleasant. Jenny would sit on the shaded side of the boat with just a light shawl around her shoulders. We met several wonderful people on the trip south. Some were our age and older and some were much younger. We knew of at least two couples on their honeymoon. I was amazed at the quality of the food we had on the boat. We were served southern fried chicken on several occasions, and I had to admit it was even better than Jenny`s. We had steak, ham, rabbit, pork, fish and a variety of spaghetti dishes. Every meal was followed by tasty desserts and coffee or tea. Every afternoon around three, more pastries and pies were placed on the forward deck for any who cared to partake.

At night we were entertained by a group of singers and musicians who were quite good. The card room provided the opportunity for games of chance for those wishing to participate. I had never played any poker but enjoyed watching some of the games. As little as I knew, it seemed to me that the fancy dressed men who played every night were always the winners. One particular gambler, a dapper individual by the name of James Brittain Lee appeared to be the most successful. I'm not sure how he won so much, but I don't think the word 'chance' had anything to do with it.

At the end of the card room was a large wheel with numbers on it. On the table beneath it were numbers matching those on the wheel. Jenny put one dollar on # 8 and won ten dollars on the first spin. She was like a child with a new toy. She quickly put her winnings in her purse and left the room. I think she was wise as I rarely saw anyone leave the tables a winner.

We made an overnight stop at Vicksburg. The crews unloaded a lot of the livestock and took on more cotton. We were allowed to leave the boat and explore the city. Jenny and I rented a buckboard with a driver and he showed us the city and the old battlefield area. Although it had been over thirty years since the war you could still see evidence of the battle. As we looked at the terrain around Vicksburg, it was easy to see what had happened when Grant cut off all supply routes entering the city. The Confederate Army and the inhabitants of the city were left to fend for themselves. Many brave men died before Pemberton surrendered.

I thought of Spence Jenkins and how he must have suffered here. When Jenny and I had stayed at Spence and Wanda's house on our way to Memphis and he told me of his experiences in Vicksburg, I could only imagine what the former defender of Vicksburg had endured. As I looked at the place where the battle had taken place, I knew Spence and all the other brave soldiers had literally almost starved to death. I couldn't imagine anything worse. What I had seen and experienced at Fort Donelson and Shiloh were minor compared to what these men endured. I was happy when we returned to the River Queen. As the boat left the dock and moved into the channel of the Mississippi, I could feel the peace around me, and it helped to take away the horror of the scene at Vicksburg.

Late in the afternoon we passed Natchez. Many stately mansions were visible from the river. Our tour director on the boat told us that at the beginning of the war Natchez had more millionaires than any other city in the south.

On our third night out from Memphis Jenny was restless and wanted to walk around the deck. The moon was bright, and the boat was moving at a good pace down the river. We could see large trees on the banks with Spanish moss hanging from the limbs. At supper we had been informed we were now in Louisiana.

We had walked to the lower deck where most of the staff cabins were. There we saw two women standing by the rail looking out toward the eastern bank of the river. We could tell that one of the women was older than the other. Jenny spoke to them as we passed. The women were not shabbily dressed, but you could tell from their appearance they were not paying passengers. The older of the two turned to Jenny and said,

"Hello ma'am. Hope you are enjoying this beautiful evening."

Jenny was surprised by the northern brogue and the delivery from the well spoken lady. Jenny stopped and engaged the ladies in conversation. What Jenny found out from the two ladies that night on the Mississippi would start a chain reaction that would change our lives forever.

I said my gentlemanly hello's and stood back to let Jenny do all the talking. The older Ladies name was Stuart Moses and her daughter's name was Alicia. The two ladies had been in Memphis for five years and worked at odd jobs on the docks. They took in laundry and did heavy labor loading wagons. They had secured jobs on the boat as dishwashers two years past. The longer Jenny talked to the ladies the more sordid the story got. Jenny found that the area around the docks in Memphis was a haven for women from several states who had migrated down the river after the war. Many had prostituted themselves to travelers and workers on the boats. They had forced their daughters into the trade, when they themselves were no longer young enough to be attractive to the customers. This happened to Stuart when she was a young lady. To keep Alicia from falling into the profession Stuart had taken jobs on the boats to make enough money to live in one of the run down shacks south of the docks. I had seen these deplorable buildings and couldn't imagine anyone actually living in them.

Jenny had Stuart and Alicia sit with us on the deck chairs so the conversation could continue. As we sat there for over two hours, we pieced together a story that was quite hard to believe. We realized, however, there would have been no reason for Mrs. Moses to tell us a lie about her past.

It seems that back in '61 when the war started, Stuart's mother had been a working prostitute in Philadelphia. After war broke out she took eighteen year old Stuart with her and the two became 'Camp Followers'. Stuart's mother and two other prostitutes purchased a covered wagon and two horses for forty dollars. They converted it to a traveling brothel. They first met the troops at the First Battle of Bull Run. They would place their wagon alongside eight or ten others, and the men in the Union Army would pay them one to three dollars for their favors. As the youngest and prettiest, Stuart was the most popular girl in the small wagon train. She could command the full three dollars and in some weeks she made as much as eighty five dollars.

This lifestyle would continue throughout the war. As the soldiers broke camp, the ladies would follow. Stuart said that on some occasions they had even been near the battles. She related that at Chancellorsville they got too close to the encampment and were almost over run by Confederates as they attacked. Stuart said she could see the faces of the southern boys as they raced by not fifty yards from their wagon.

When the war ended, Stuart and her mother moved to St. Louis. They heard traffic on the river was heavy and 'ladies of the night' would have no trouble finding customers. While in St. Louis, Stuart's mother became ill and passed away. Stuart wasn't sure, but she assumed her mother had contracted some social disease from one of her customers.

Stuart said she had always tried to be careful but in 1878 she discovered she was going to have a child. She had no idea who the father was. It could have been any one of the scores of men she had been with the past year. When she found out she was pregnant, she vowed to never prostitute herself again. She took any job she could on the river boats, and when Alicia was born, she saved enough to rent a small place by the docks and raise her child.

Stuart said life at St. Louis had been tolerable until five years ago when a ladies group came to the docks and put up signs demanding prostitutes and former prostitutes leave the city. Pressure from the crusading ladies had been so fierce that Stuart had taken thirteen year old Alicia on one of the boats and got off at Memphis. At first, life in Memphis wasn't too bad. She got a job as a cook in one of the small café's by the river and the proprietor let she and Alicia live above café in a small apartment. Alicia had always gone to school and was quite bright.

Stuart said the trouble came when a customer in the café recognized her. He made lewd remarks to her about their past experiences, and when the owner of the café realized that his cook was a former prostitute, he demanded she leave that day.

Since then, Stuart and Alicia had been forced to live in the shanty town by the river with other outcast women. Stuart estimated there were at least thirty or forty homeless women and their children living in the squaller of the river shacks.

As I looked at Alicia, I could see she was an unhappy eighteen year old. While most of her peers were going to parties and dating young men, this pretty brunette was on a boat washing dishes just to exist. I couldn't condone the former life style of her mother, but this young girl had done nothing in her life to deserve her fate.

When we returned to our stateroom, Jenny was almost in tears. She was such a loving and caring person. She couldn't abide by the fact that so many women and their young were struggling to eke out some existence when we and many others had so much. I could tell then Jenny had some plans developing in her mind.

Chapter 26

We enjoyed New Orleans and the rest of our excursion, but it was obvious that Jenny's mind was on only one thing. On our trip north to Memphis, Jenny had several more conversations with Stuart Moses and her daughter, Alicia. The ladies formed a close bond, and I could see Alicia's countenance brighten when Jenny would walk up. I think Alicia somehow knew this new friend was going to make a difference in her life.

When we arrived back in Memphis, we went to see our old friend, Mr. Porter, at his real estate office. He recognized us immediately and with a broad smile on his round face walked toward us and stuck out his hand.

"Well, Mr. and Mrs. Wade. How have you been? I hope you are now very happy citizens of Memphis."

Mr. Porter was pleased that we liked our new home and our adopted city. We wasted little time in informing him of our purpose for this visit.

"Mr. Porter," said Jenny excitedly. "We want to find a roomy place where we can provide housing for several ladies and a few children. We intend to establish a residence for homeless and destitute women. We were hoping you could help us."

Mr. Porter removed his glasses and wiped them on his handkerchief. He had his head lowered and you could tell he was in deep thought. It seemed a full minute before he spoke.

"You know, Mrs. Wade. We might have just what you need. The building is quite large, however, and I fear the price would be a bit on the high side."

"Money won't be an object, Mr. Porter," said Jenny confidently.

I knew Jenny intended for Mr. Lincoln to cover all the expenses of her project.

I smiled and entered the conversation.

"I wouldn't put it quite that way, Mr. Porter, but we would be prepared to spend a tidy sum on the building if necessary."

I remembered the excitement on Mr. Porter's face when he took us to see our home last year. I saw that same look in his eyes as he rose from his chair and got his coat and hat off one of the pegs on the wall.

"Come on you two. Let's go take a look."

Mr. Porter called his wife from the back room and re-introduced us. He asked Mrs. Porter to stay in the office while he took us to see a building.

We rode in Mr. Porter's buggy about ten blocks south on front street. We were five blocks below the River View Inn where we had stayed when we first arrived in Memphis. On the East side of the street was a huge building with a "For Sale" sign on the door. Mr. Porter told us the building had been a cotton warehouse during the war, and the owners had lost it to the bank. There had been some talk of crooked dealings by one of the partners. Rumors said the man left the country with all of the company's assets. The Union Planters Bank of Memphis was forced to foreclose on the remaining partners for failure to meet the loan payments.

When I first looked at the building, I thought it much too large and not structured for housing. I could see Jenny's eyes brighten however. She urged Mr. Porter to let us see the inside.

The building, although probably fifty years old was quite sound structurally. I estimated the building to be about sixty feet wide and one hundred feet deep. There were three floors, with sturdy stairs going to each floor. There was also an elevator in the rear with an ingenious system of pulleys that lifted the carriage quite easily from floor to floor by simply pulling some ropes. Mr. Porter pointed out that the building was sturdy enough so walls could be assembled at any location and rooms could be put in whatever sizes desired. The building had been electrified some time ago. When we lowered the lever on the main power box lights came on from wires hanging from the ceiling.

"I know a local contractor who could come in here and do whatever we cared to do to make the place not only livable but quite nice," said Mr. Porter. He got more excited about the project as he talked, and his enthusiasm rubbed off on Jenny.

Without speaking, Jenny walked up the stairs to the second and then the third floors. Each floor was a mirror image of the other except the top floor had glass in a portion of the ceiling to let light in. The floors were a good quality hard wood with a waxy finish on the wood.

"How much is the building?" asked Jenny. "And how much do you think it would cost to add walls, two bathrooms on each floor and lights in each room."

Mr. Porter slowly walked around, took out a pad and jotted some things down. He might not have known much about building projects, but he made us think he did. He didn't speak for at least five minutes and then turned to us and said,

"Well, the bank wants $50,000 for the building, and that's a bargain. I understand this is what was owed when the company folded. As to the work to get the place like you want it. I think Mr. Shackleford would want at least $10,000 per floor. We worked together on a warehouse down by the train station last year. This project will be similar and I feel the ten thousand per floor would be pretty accurate. I feel the total of your project would be right at $80,000. That would be fifty for the building and thirty for the work."

I knew we still had over three hundred thousand of Mr. Lincoln's dollars back at the farm. I knew the price Mr. Porter was proposing wouldn't be a problem. Jenny looked at me and when she saw my smile she didn't hesitate.

"We'll take it!" she said. "When can we start?"

Mr. Porter was taken aback by Jenny's statement. He knew his commission on the sale would be a tidy sum and he was obviously pleased.

"We will have to clear the purchase with the bank and have Mr. Shackleford consult with you on your desires. I would suggest you get his draftsman to come with you here to the building and come up with some preliminary plans. I would think we could start the project in two to three weeks."

Jenny was really excited and wanted to share the news of our project with Jed and Molly. We boarded the train for Corinth on the 5th of May and visited with the children for a couple days in

Iuka. The trip gave me opportunity to get the necessary gold for the project. I deposited forty thousand dollars with the Bank of Iuka and another forty at the Southern Trust Bank in Corinth. I didn`t want all that gold with me while we were traveling. Jenny and I carried ten thousand on our persons, and it wasn`t difficult. The people at the bank in Iuka and also at Corinth showed no special emotion when we placed all the gold coins on the counter. Gold was in heavy use in the country. Many businesses did all their transactions with gold coins. Everywhere we went we were accepted as well to do land owners and merchants. Thanks to Mr. Lincoln the deception was easy to carry off.

We closed the deal with Union Planters Bank and got a clear deed for the building. The $50,000 included a nice parking area at the rear of the building for wagons and a roomy stable for horses. I knew with a little work I could get the stable in good condition. We showed Mr. Shackleford, our contractor, what we wanted. He suggested four bathrooms on each floor as there would be so many people using them. He divided each floor into four sections with hallways going down the middle and a crossing hallway in the center. He decided to put a small kitchen in each apartment with a larger, better equipped kitchen on the main floor where group meals could be prepared. Heat to the rooms would be provided by a new steam system with radiators in each room. Mr. Shackleford was a brilliant man and knew his business quite well. He carried us to the building he had completed near Central Station and showed us the type rooms he had done there. Our project would be much larger, but the room arrangements would be similar.

After much planning and decision making, Mr. Shackleford gave us a finished price of $26,000 to put rooms and baths on all of the three floors.

We were quite pleased with the price. Work started in late May. Jenny informed Stuart Moses of our plans and told Stuart we would like for she and her daughter, Alicia to be the managers of the building for us. We would provide them an apartment on the first floor and give them a salary each month for seeing about the property. Stuart and Alicia were elated. They came over to the building almost daily during construction and made many suggestions as things progressed.

Jenny had personally visited all the ladies in the shacks by the river and informed them of the new housing that would be provided for them. Jenny was quite clear to them that there would be certain rules that would be adhered to in the building. I was quite proud of what I called Jenny's Ten Commandments for the new home.

1. No alcohol of any kind on the premises.
2. No tobacco products including snuff and cigars.
3. Men visitors were welcome, but must leave the building by 10:00 P.M.
4. Weekly baths are required for all residents including children.
5. Clothing must be neat and modest at all times.
6. Each resident must work their fair share of time in the laundry and kitchen.
7. Church attendance is required. Transportation will be provided.
8. Each adult will diligently seek gainful and reputable employment.
9. All employed residents will pay $20 per month to help defray expenses.
10. Residents are encouraged to interact with their neighbors and live as a large family.

Stuart, Alicia and Jenny had drafted the rules, and Stuart felt they were reasonable. Some of the women hadn't lived in any real home in years and regulations as to life style were necessary. Unwritten, but clearly a part of the rules was that prostitution of any type must end on the day the resident entered the home. Any resident found to be continuing this practice would be asked to leave. Each potential resident would be personally interviewed by Stuart or Jenny. Jenny's wish was to get as many homeless and destitute women off the streets as possible. She had no desire, however, to put a potential trouble maker in the building.

Chapter 27

Before the building work was completed in August, Jenny, Stuart and Alicia canvassed the downtown business community. They informed the proprietors of the new home and the desire to secure employment for all the residents. Many of the businesses agreed to interview the ladies. The owners thought the idea was sound and would be an asset to the city.

I personally visited all the downtown churches and let them know of the project. In all cases, the news was received with joy and praise. Some church leaders even agreed to help and provide food, clothing, bedding and other supplies for the project. A ladies group at the First Methodist Church said they would make weekly visits and offer singing and other entertainment while counseling with the ladies at the home.
The Men's Club at the Catholic Church said they would provide all needed buggies, and drivers, to take the ladies at the home to the church of their choice each Sunday.
Three doctors at our Baptist Church agreed to give the ladies free medical examinations and treatment if illness was found. One of the men specialized in treating children. He said he would visit the home personally and examine all the children in their own rooms.

By the time the home opened, we had filled all of the available apartments. There were twelve apartments on each of the top two floors and eight on the first, including Stuart and Alicia's. In all we started with thirty seven women and thirteen children. Eight of the women had a grown daughter living with them. Of all the residents at the home Stuart feared trouble from these eight young ladies more than anyone else. Stuart knew that in all cases except her own Alicia, these girls had been practicing prostitutes. Most of them since they were as young as fourteen.   These poor girls had never known anything but to be used by men and had not experienced true love in their entire lives. Of special concern to Stuart was Polly Grimes. Polly was not totally happy to move into the home and only did so at the insistence of her mother. Polly was seventeen, and it was easy to see she bore watching. Alicia had known Polly and said of all the girls on the river Polly was the only one who seemed to like her profession. Polly was more developed than the other girls and never had trouble finding her a willing client for the night. Stuart and Alicia knew they would have to keep a close eye on this good looking, defiant teenager.

Jenny decided to name the home after her mother. The Mayor of Memphis was on hand on August 25th when the Agnes Swanson Home for Ladies was opened. The mayor said a few words of encouragement, and in a flowery way thanked Jenny for her gracious generosity. The mayor told the crowd he had instructed the city work crew to burn all the shacks by the river and build a scenic park in the area. The mayor asked Jenny if she would like to name the new park. Jenny didn't have to think on this. She immediately said she would like to see it called, "Lincoln Park.."

I had to suppress a smile as I knew the significance of this strange request from a southern lady from Mississippi. After all, Mr. Lincoln had made all of this possible by letting us use his gold and it was only right that he should be honored in some small way.

By opening day most of the ladies had been employed by merchants in town. A few had taken jobs at some of the cotton warehouses on Front Street. Stuart was wonderful with the ladies. She understood what they had experienced in their lives and knew most of the ladies only needed a chance to better themselves. Stuart also knew rarely if ever had any of these women chosen prostitution. It had usually been forced on them by parents and other relatives.

The ladies at the home were accepted without question by the local churches. Many had never been to church and some could only remember attending as children. Alicia coordinated the transportation with the Catholic Men, and on most Sundays there would be six to eight carriages at the front door waiting to transport the ladies and their children to the church of their choice.

The women of the local First Presbyterian Church came by the home and outfitted all the ladies with nice Sunday clothes. On the first Sunday of September, I looked at the ladies climbing in the carriages, and thought I was watching Memphis' high society leaving for a grand ball.

Jenny rarely spent time at our house. We were only about fifteen blocks from the Ladies Home and she would have me hook the horse to the wagon for her ten minute ride.

Stella Watkins, our next door neighbor was invaluable to us during these days. She had visited the Ladies Home and knew how important it was for Jenny to be there on most days. She watered our flowers, swept the porch and generally kept the place looking quite nice while we were so busy. Having such a wonderful neighbor was a special joy to Jenny.

Jenny had always been quite comfortable on a horse and on pretty days rode her faithful mare, Suzy. She preferred to ride on my conventional saddle. Being a well thought of lady in Memphis, however, she relented. She started using her side saddle so she could wear her long skirts instead of the heavy trousers she had always preferred back home in Iuka.

She found that by going straight to Front Street from the house she had little problem turning south. The wagon and buggy traffic was so heavy on Main Street, Jenny avoided it whenever possible.

I accompanied Jenny to the Ladies Home on most days. There were usually a few things to do that were best suited for a man. It wasn't long until I realized we would need a full time man working at the place. I was pretty good with usual chores but wasn't much with plumbing problems. I also hated cleaning floors and windows. Each of the occupants took care of the floors in their own apartments, but the halls were very large and took almost continuous care.

I was sweeping the front steps one clear October morning. I stepped on a loose board and twisted my ankle. I was in a pretty foul mood and shouted a loud, "Damn". I looked toward the river and saw a lone colored man approaching. He asked if he could be of any assistance. After a short conversation I learned that the man had worked his way down the river from St. Louis and was looking for a job. I tried not to show my joy. I went through the motions of asking various questions about the man knowing full well he had gotten the job the minute he walked up those steps.

Webster Sample was about my age and looked in good physical condition. His clothes were becoming threadbare, but the man was clean and well spoken. It was obvious he was not a southern Negro as his speech sounded more northern. He didn't impress me as a man who had much formal schooling, but something about him made me like him instantly. His handshake was firm and although he didn't act humble or subservient, he was very careful to answer all questions with "yes sir" and "no sir" when the occasion called for it. I didn't know this man's past, but something told me it was a good thing fate sent him to us at just the right time.

Webster told me most people simply called him Web. Web was slightly taller than I at about six feet. He had no extra meat on his bones and appeared well muscled. I knew he would be able to handle any duty required at the home.

Web had a terrible scar at the hairline just above his left eye extending backward and down to his ear. Some serious injury had occurred in this dark skinned man's life to cause such a mar to an otherwise nice looking face.

I showed Web around the place and took him to the tack room at the livery stable where he would live. I introduced Web to Jenny, and we agreed we would pay him forty dollars a month and provide him with all his meals. I purchased some new clothes for Web and his necessary bedding.

Web Sample proved to be a an Angel in disguise. He could do anything. He repaired broken windows and doors. He could unstop clogged pipes and was very adept at keeping the place clean.

The ladies of the home took an immediate liking to Webster. I could feel that he would be a real asset in the event of trouble. Web Sample didn't appear to me to be a man who would run from any fight if he thought the cause right.

The children in the home adored Web. He would spend countless hours playing with them. The mothers soon found they could leave the children with Webster and know they would be well cared for.

Web was especially good with horses. I soon found out why. In one of our evening discussions over a cup of coffee I found that Webster Sample had served in the Union Cavalry during the war. He had run away from a run down orphanage in Philadelphia when he was fifteen and joined the Union Army. No one had ever questioned his age, and he spent the entire war in campaigns in and around Virginia and Washington D. C.. After the war he had joined General Phil Sheridan in the 9th Cavalry Corps in the Indian Campaigns out west. He told me a little about some of his battles with the Indians but was reluctant to carry the discussions too far.

Webster mustered out of the army in 1888 when he was forty four years old. Washington sent orders that men over forty and not yet officers would be asked to resign from the army to make room for younger recruits. Webster had been devastated. He told me he knew nothing but Army life and had nowhere to go. He tried St. Louis for seven years but never really liked the place. He lived with a woman for a year before she left with a trapper heading west. He had done all type jobs while in St. Louis but decided to travel south and see if life could be a little better for him.

I had a special feeling for my new black friend and was determined to do what I could to see he was happy in his new surroundings. I could only imagine what things still haunted the mind of Webster Sample. It was evident that something in his past was quite troublesome to him.

Chapter 28

Polly Grimes didn't come back from Church on Sunday, the third week of March, 1897. Her mother said she sensed Polly was unhappy in the home and wanted to leave. She told of finding a note from a renegade gambler off one of the river boats urging Polly to join him and explore life on the river.

Webster and I made inquiries at the docks and put together a pretty good picture of what had occurred. Some of the workers had seen Polly arrive in Slats Hansford's buggy and had seen Slats and her enter the boat together. Other stories told of seeing them together in Vicksburg and later at New Orleans. The couple evidently left the boat and were living somewhere in or around the docks in the Louisiana city.

Polly was now eighteen and had selected this lifestyle for herself. Her mother was saddened but understood. She knew when she was Polly's age if she had been given the opportunity to leave the trade and be taken care of by a well to do man she would have done it instantly. She just hoped the infamous Slats Hansford didn't dump her daughter for another and leave Polly to fend for herself again.

Such was life at the home. Most of the ladies had become decent, law abiding citizens and an asset to the community. Many met and married men of the town, and two of the ladies saved enough money to open Two Sisters, an upscale dress shop just off Main Street on Poplar Avenue near the park.

Stuart and Alicia had no trouble filling any vacancies that occurred. The river provided an unrestricted flow of destitute women. The reputation of the Agnes Swanson Home for Ladies had spread from St. Louis to New Orleans.

The first gasoline powered car I ever saw arrived at the door of the home in September of 1904. Mayor Thomas and two of his staff pulled up in one of the strange contraptions and offered to take Jenny and me for a ride. I had read with interest in the papers about the advent of the horseless machines but wasn't prepared for my reaction on actually seeing one. After our ride of about thirty minutes, I knew

I had to have one of these remarkable vehicles for my very own. I paid the outrageous sum of eight hundred dollars for a new Ford and knew my life, and actually the lives of all the people in the world had been changed by this fantastic machine. By the summer of 1905 hundreds of the motor driven automobiles were regularly driving the streets of Memphis.

The advent of the automobile brought immediate changes to the economy of the city. Work crews were brought in from throughout the land to prepare the carriage roads for the much faster gasoline vehicles. Businesses related to the sale and care of the automobile popped up all over town. Memphis was no longer a sleepy cotton town on the bluff. It was now a thriving river city with an adequate port to receive and ship automobiles throughout the land. With the added wealth and business came more and more saloons, bars and dance halls. Our ladies at the home had many opportunities to return to their former lives, but in most cases, they not only stayed but tried to keep other hapless girls off the streets. On some nights Web prepared cots in the halls and several homeless girls new to the city would take advantage of the offer to rest, take a bath, and enjoy a hot meal. We simply didn't have room for all the ladies who were pouring into the city each month.

The home became self sufficient by the fall of 1905. Jenny felt the need to expand.

We had given away a few of Mr. Lincoln's gold coins to needy people through the years but we had left most of that enterprise in the hands of Jed and Molly. I had long ago taken most of the remaining coins from their hiding places behind the farm in Iuka and distributed it all in various banks in Mississippi and Tennessee. The interest alone on the remaining $200,000 amounted to almost six thousand dollars a year. This was more than enough for Jenny and me to live very comfortably in our home in Memphis.

Jenny contacted the Mayor and convinced him of the need to start another home for ladies. The Mayor's wife was receptive to the idea and urged her husband to ask the city father's to give Jenny Swanson a vacant building for another home and to provide workers and materials to get the home in good condition.

Two adjoining buildings three blocks south of our first ladies home on Front Street had been abandoned since around 1890. The city had taken them over for unpaid taxes. They were not only an eye sore but a drain on the city workers who tried to keep the buildings in some state of repair. With spit, polish and hard work, we opened the second Agnes Swanson Ladies Home in March of 1906. Webster Sanders had married a former river boat cook, Martha Hankins. He and his wife became caretakers of the new home. Webster had become such a fixture in Memphis that most people forgot he was black.

Webster and I met regularly for our private time over a cup of coffee, and as time moved on Web opened up a little to me about his exploits in the war and as an Indian fighter. I had heard the term "Buffalo Soldier" but really never knew what it meant. As Web and I talked further, I found that the name had been given to the colored Cavalry Regiments by the Indians they were fighting.

I knew nothing at all about the struggles of our soldiers on the western frontier, and I always listened with interest as Webster told of some of his battles. He never mentioned the scar on his face and head. I respected his privacy and never pressed the issue. At times I would sense that Web had some experiences in his past he simply wanted to forget and never talk about. I cared so much for this dark skinned friend I let him always decide how much to tell me.

9th CAVALRY- U. S. ARMY- NEW MEXICO TERRITORY- 1879

Sergeant Webster Sample had served in the 9th Cavalry for fourteen years since the Civil War. He had seen numerous battles against various tribes of Indians from Texas to the Dakota's. So successful were the troops of the 9th Cavalry that the hostile Indians of the Plains had given the all colored regiment the name, ' Buffalo Soldiers'. Most Apaches had never seen a black man before and were impressed no end by the skill and daring of the dark skinned Union soldiers. .

Orders from Washington had decreed that all the Apache tribes would be concentrated in reservations in and around San Carlos, Arizona. This desolate wasteland was despised by all Apaches. The independent lifestyle and culture of the Apaches and their hatred of the San Carlos reservation insured that hostilities would occur. The renegade Apaches that periodically fled the reservations were highly skilled horsemen with a superior knowledge of their ancestral lands. Under the command of warriors like Skinya, Nana, Victorio and Geronimo, the Apaches proved to be an illusive and worthy adversary.

Company C and Company F was assigned guard duty along the Las Asimas Creek in the Black Range of New Mexico. Wagon trains were regularly attacked by marauding Apaches and many white women and children had been captured.

Lieutenant Jordan Smythe was ordered to take Company C into the hills and secure the release of three white women known to be held by the Warm Springs Apaches and their War Chief, Victorio. Scouts spotted some of Victorio's warriors at a buffalo kill on September 16th and had watched them return to their campground with much needed fresh meat. The scouts felt they had not been seen by the Apaches but such was not the case. The warriors had indeed spotted the scouts and prepared an ambush for any approaching Union Cavalry.

Lieutenant Smythe assigned the point position to his most experienced non- commissioned officer, Sergeant Webster Sanders.

155

Sergeant Sanders and thirteen troopers advanced through a draw between two steep bluffs and were cut off from behind by more than forty armed Apaches. Four of Sergeant Sanders' men were killed in the first attack but the men were able to dismount and form a defensive position behind some boulders and hold off the attackers. More Apaches attacked from the north opening of the draw.

Fighting was fierce for over thirty minutes. The expert marksmen of the Buffalo Soldiers killed over twenty of the Apaches. Only the sheer numbers of the Indians allowed the men of Company C to be overrun. Men on both sides fought bravely with knives, bayonets and rifles. Sergeant Sanders recognized the man he thought to be Victorio. Victorio hadn't gained the reputation as his fellow war chief, Geronimo, but those who had seen Victorio's handiwork knew him to be ruthless and brutal to any and all whites. Victorio killed for the love of killing, and when he captured Union Cavalrymen he made their last hours of life as miserable as possible. One of Victorio's favorite tortures was to remove the fingers on each hand one at a time until the screaming soldier died from loss of blood. Victorio had even been known to scalp young girls, and had been seen carrying the small blond hairpieces on his lance.

Webster Sanders raised his Winchester `73 repeater to his shoulder and aimed squarely at the heart of Victorio only to find his gun empty. Victorio saw his advantage and rode full gallop toward Sergeant Sanders. In one move he vaulted from his horse, raised his knife and cut sharply trying to scalp Web Sanders with one swift blow. Web only had time to move his head slightly to his left. The razor sharp knife took off the skin over the left eye and back toward his ear. Sergeant Sanders fell unconscious to the ground. Victorio raised his knife to finish his task when the sound of an Army bugle startled him. As he stood, he saw the charging horses of the remainder of Company's C and F under the command of Lieutenant Smythe. Victorio remounted his horse and led his men back up the ravine and into the mountains leaving what was left of Sergeant Sanders and his decimated platoon.

Of the thirteen men who had entered the ravine only four were still alive. All others had been killed, and six of the dead had been scalped.

Lieutenant Smythe led his entire force into the hills and found the Apache's had abandoned their camp. They found two of the captured women who had been tied naked to stakes but were both still alive. It was evident to all that the women had been ravaged by numerous Apaches and neither could tell the fate of the other woman. The two women were returned to their families. The third white woman was never found.

Sergeant Webster Sanders would recover from his horrendous wounds and fight in numerous encounters with the Apaches, but he never saw Victorio again. He was transferred to Fort Riley, Kansas in 1882 and was at the fort when word came that Victorio and Geronimo had been captured. The Apaches had looted, raided, plundered, raped and killed for twenty years, but with the capture of the two most notorious War Chiefs, the battles with the Plains Indians virtually ended.

During his four years in fighting for the North in the War Between the States, Webster Sanders saw many terrible battles. He was wounded at Richmond and had been in two hand to hand battles with Rebel Infantry at Sharpsburg and Charlotsville. Many nights as Web Sanders tried to sleep, the vision of charging, screaming Rebels caused him alarm. The most haunting memory of all however, was the sight of a bronze skinned warrior with blazing black eyes leaping from his charging horse and raising his knife to slice away the top of his scalp. It was a nightmare he couldn't shake from his memory.

Chapter 29

By November of 1908 Webster Sanders and I had become best friends. His attitude and demeanor were exemplary, and all who came in contact with him at the second Agnes Swanson Ladies Home were quite impressed by the quiet, yet very efficient colored man.

One of the ladies reported at supper one evening she saw a man looking at her through the outside window of her apartment. Webster heard of the incident and laid in wait to catch the peeping Tom. One cool evening right after Thanksgiving, Web saw the man standing on a box and peering into the bathroom window at one of the ladies taking her bath.

"Hey, you white trash. Get your butt away from that window before I knocks you away," hollered Web at the top of his voice.

"You talking to me you black, Yankee bastard," answered the man.

Web grabbed the culprit by the collar and seat of his pants and literally threw him out into the street.

"You come back here and look at another of these ladies, and I'll cut your throat from one ear to the other," said Web, quite emphatically.

The startled man realized he had met more than his match and scurried down the street to safety. He wanted no part of this powerful dark skinned man.

When the ladies heard of the incident Web became an instant celebrity around the place. The children started calling him Uncle Web. Webster loved it. I knew he would gladly give his life in the defense of these white women and their children under his care.

After we reported the incident to the local police, one of the mounted patrolmen made regular visits in the alley behind the ladies home. No other occurrence was noticed. Evidently Web had made a lasting impression on our lone offender.

On Sunday afternoons Web and I spent many hours walking the banks of the Mississippi and sharing stories of our pasts. I told him about Shiloh. Web assumed I had fought for the Confederacy. I never told anyone outside the family about my being a Union soldier but for some reason I shared the story with Webster. I let Web know of my dismay when I first saw men firing at each other at Fort Henry. I told of my abhorrence with war and how I had vowed never to point a gun at another human in anger. I related the story of leaving the field of battle at Shiloh and eventually making my way to Iuka. I lied to Webster about our wealth. I told him Jenny and I made our money in land and cotton. I trusted Web but knew the secret of Mr. Lincoln's Gold was too important to tell anyone. Although we had been careful to use most of the money to help others, I had no doubt as to my fate if the true story of the gold got to the Federal Authorities. It bothered me to lie to my best friend but felt I had no other choice in the matter.

I was taken aback by Webster's reaction to my story. He said he had killed scores of men in his life and he hated every one of the experiences. He even regretted killing the hostile Indians. He told me how poorly the Sioux, Apaches and other tribes had been treated by our government and the deplorable conditions they were forced into. He knew if he had been in their place he would have fought for his land and family just as Victorio and Geronimo had.

As sunset settled over the Mississippi, I felt for my trusted friend. I knew he had always done his duty and followed the orders of his superiors, but in most cases he did not like the outcome. As we watched the beauty of the evening approach talking ceased. We had both shared our souls with the other and the memories of long ago days began to crowd our memory. We must have sat by the river for another thirty minutes before we knew it was time to join the ladies at supper.

I invited Web to sit with us at one of the tables in the dining room, but he declined. He and his wife always had their meals at the small table in the main kitchen. Web never made a move around the home that would be misunderstood by any of the ladies, particularly the younger women. He knew he had been accepted as a friend, but he was still a colored man among white people and even in his native north this was less than a desirable situation. I felt for my friend but respected his desires. I never raised my hand in anger at another man since Shiloh, but I knew now if anyone ever tried to harm Web Sanders they would have to deal with us both. I also knew the ladies of the home would be right there beside me.

Webster and his wife came up with several ideas to help the newer ladies adjust to life in the Ladies home. The second home where Web and his wife were now living was larger than the first and had an enormous dining room to the rear of the first floor. Web and his wife, Martha, got the ladies to organize special socials at least once a month and would invite the inhabitants of the original home to participate. Favorite events were spelling contests between the two homes, taffy pulls, quilting parties, group singing and tacky parties. I will never forget seeing some of the outfits the ladies came up with at the first tacky party. It was the intention that the ladies look as awful as possible and many succeeded beyond their dreams. The children loved the parties, and I could see a special bond form between the inhabitants of both homes.

Jenny and I knew we had done virtually all we could for the ladies. Through special arrangements with the Mayor and his wife, we deeded the property of both homes to the city of Memphis. The Mayor and his Council took over the operating expenses of both Agnes Swanson Ladies Homes. Although they were almost self sufficient, it was obvious with the services available through the city the homes would always be in good repair and never want for the niceties of life. The stable was torn down, and a large garage was built to house four automobiles that were always at the disposal of the ladies when needed. I would make regular visits to check on things and was amused that Webster not only refused to drive one of the contraptions but to my knowledge never even rode in one. He kept his favorite horse and was allowed to board him in a private stall behind the second home.

Jenny never lost her zeal for the ladies. She spent most every Sunday afternoon patrolling the dock area making sure some "fallen lady" wasn`t trying to eke out an existence by prostituting herself up and down the river. The city assigned mounted policemen to the docks, and any lady caught trying to solicit customers was arrested and carried to a holding cell where they would wait until Jenny or one of the ladies from the Home could come and rescue the unfortunate soul.

I lost count of the ladies Jenny helped to a better life but as I saw the progress made by so many at the homes I was even more convinced that Mr. Lincoln's Gold had been used in a special way and lives had been changed for the better because of it.

Chapter 30

I never felt I was an old man, but as I sat in our parlor reading the Memphis Appeal the date August 1st, 1911 caused me to turn my eyes to my wife of 48 years. Jenny and I had been through so much in those years. I cherished the memory of them all. The children back in Iuka were all grown. We had seen them regularly through the years. Jed was independently wealthy and had donated a lot of the furniture in the Agnes Swanson Ladies Homes. Molly was serving her third term as Chairman of the Woman's Missionary Union at the Baptist Church in Iuka.. Jed had been asked to run for Congress, and I had a feeling that if he did he would be elected.

At 69 I was now the second oldest member of the Men's Bible Class at our church. I still felt fine, and other than the fact I couldn't walk quite as far as I used to I think I was doing very well. As I continued to read the paper I stopped at a headline on the second page that read,

"Shiloh Battlefield to hold Fiftieth Anniversary Celebration of The Great Battle of 1862"

As I read, I saw that veterans from over twenty states were planning to convene at Pittsburg Landing the first week of April to commemorate the fighting that occurred on the 6th and 7th of April, 1862. I remembered the Government passed legislation back in 1894 to establish Military Parks at some of the biggest battle sights of the war. I knew Shiloh and Vicksburg had been selected, and I told Jenny that some day I wanted to visit Shiloh again. I knew this was the opportunity I had been looking for.

At the bottom of the page there were several ads placed in the paper by many of the states who had men who fought at Shiloh. Some of the ads were reminding men of various Army regiments to try to get to Shiloh for the celebration in April. A few of the ads were asking for donations to help build monuments recognizing the service

of men from various states.   One ad in particular caused me to pause
and read every word carefully.

THE SOVEREIGN STATE OF ILLINOIS WILL ERECT
A STIRRING MONUMENT TO THE MEMORY OF THE
EIGHT THOUSAND ILLINOIS SOLDIERS WHO GAVE
THEIR LIVES IN THE TRAGIC BATTLE AT SHILOH.
GOVERNOR BATES IS ASKING ALL FORMER SOLDIERS
AND INTERESTED PARTIES TO HELP IN THE FUNDING OF
THE MEMORIAL.   THE COST OF THE MONUMENT WILL BE
$150,000.   THOSE WISHING TO DONATE TO THE GREAT
CAUSE ARE URGED TO MAIL THEIR CONTRIBUTIONS TO
'SHILOH MEMORIAL COMMITTEE- 376 SHORELINE ROAD
CHICAGO, ILLINOIS'

As I read and re-read the notice, I knew I had found what needed
be done with the remainder of Mr. Lincoln's Gold. I called Jenny and
read her the article. Jenny looked me in the eye and in her special
way said,

"If you hadn't been a member of the Union Army from Illinois, I
would never have met you, and what we have accomplished in our
lives would not have been possible."

Jenny was now crying as she sat by me and put her head on my
shoulder. She continued.

"Mr. Lincoln was from Illinois, and I can think of no better way
for us to use his money than to give to the monument. You and I have
more than we will ever need and at our age I think it's about time we
got out of the gold business."

I hugged Jenny and wiped her tears with my handkerchief. I knew
I had made up my mind to give the money for the monument, but it
was wonderful hearing Jenny reaffirm my decision.

It took a little doing, but I went to the six banks where we had
money on deposit and had them all send a cashier's check for $25,000
to the monument committee. The banks agreed to send the money
with the simple statement-   "Donor unknown" on each check. Each
bank thought we had given just the $25,000, not knowing of the other
five checks that were sent.

Some time later, I read in the paper where the Illinois Monument Committee announced their goal of $150,000 had been over subscribed by twenty thousand dollars, and the extra money would be put in an account for the express purpose of maintaining the monument and grounds in the future. I couldn't have been more pleased.

Jenny and I found that the dedication would be on Sunday the 6th of April, 1912. We immediately started making plans to attend.

The fall of 1911 was a tragic time for the City of Memphis. The great influenza epidemic that had ravaged the country for the past year arrived with terrible swiftness in October. Hundreds of people of all ages were struck down by the terrible disease. People would start out with simply a common cold, but when the fever set in, many went into convulsions and died within three days. Small children and the aged were particularly hard hit. Hardly a family escaped without some loved one succumbing to the flu.

Local doctors said they thought the sickness was brought to Memphis from the river traffic. All the northern cities on the river had already experienced serious outbreaks. It was assumed people traveling on the river boats infected locals as they came in contact on the docks, in restaurants, churches and businesses. It seems the disease was easily passed from person to person.

Jenny and I helped all we could with the sick, and for some reason never got so much as a cough. We lost a lot of close friends, however. Mr. Porter, the friendly and helpful real estate agent, was one of the first to pass away. He had been such a help to us and had donated a lot of his time to the ladies homes. We saw a black ribbon on the door of the office on Main Street and found out from the ladies shop next door that Mr. Porter and his wife both died the second week of October. We felt as if we had lost a member of our family.

Four of the children and two of the women at the ladies homes also passed away as a result of the influenza. Notices came out daily in the paper with instructions in the use of heavy cleaners. People were told to wear masks around the face if any contact were to be made with anyone who already had the Flu.

Business virtually came to a stand still in the city, and on many days you would see no one on the streets.

We didn't travel to Iuka during the flu outbreak as we were afraid we would somehow infect the children. We planned for the kids to visit us at Thanksgiving and to take the grandchildren on an overnight boat trip up to St. Louis, but we decided against it. Too many young adults in Tennessee were getting the disease. By the middle of November there had been only spotty reports of the flu in Mississippi. We didn't want to take any chances.

As quickly as the disease arrived, it left in December. We had an unusually cold spell around the 10th. After that it was rare to hear of any new cases of the Flu. Doctors weren't sure but they felt the cold weather somehow killed the germs that caused the disease or at least kept it from spreading further. The city had been scarred and battered but as the Mayor said in the paper,

"We have weathered the terrible Influenza epidemic and although many of our fine citizens have gone on to their glory the city remains strong and vibrant. I urge all Memphians to look to your neighbors and do what you can to ease the burden of the loss of a loved one. Memphis has survived and as we offer our condolences and prayers to our friends we send a clarion call to all who will hear. Memphis is alive and well again. We have been wounded but not beaten. We will never forget the hundreds who lost their lives, and it is with their memory in mind that we declare that Memphis will be an even greater city than before."

The Mayor's letter seemed to lift the people's spirits, and by Christmas the city was bustling again. We checked with our personal doctor. He agreed it would be all right for us to go to Iuka and see the children. We always tried to spend Christmas back home on the farm. Jed would laugh and tell us he really never got a birthday present. Since he was born on Christmas day, he said all we ever did was hold out one of his Christmas presents and put Happy Birthday on it.

We drove our Ford to Iuka, and on the way decided to stop by and see Wanda and Spence Jenkins. We had only seen them the one time on our first trip to Memphis but they had become special friends.

As we parked in the Jenkins yard we noticed how much better the place looked. It had been a pretty dreary place sixteen years before when we accepted Wanda and Spence's hospitality and spent the night with them.

Wanda was bringing in eggs from the barn when we approached the porch and she recognized us immediately. She placed the eggs on the ground and ran to Jenny. The two friends hugged and Wanda couldn't hold back the tears.

"Oh, Jenny! How I have longed to see you all these years. What you did for us changed our lives."

We knew Wanda was referring to the thousand dollars we left on their kitchen table back in '95. I removed my hat and gave Wanda a kiss on the cheek.

"You look great, Wanda," I said. "How is Spence?"

Wanda smiled, lowered her head and quietly said.

"He fought hard, Marcus, but his lungs finally gave out. He died in October, 1906."

We offered our condolences, but Wanda was quick to point out how wonderful Spence's last years had been. Their son, Walt, had purchased four milk cows with some of Mr. Lincoln's Gold. The herd had grown through the years to fourteen animals and they produced enough quality milk for Wanda to have a comfortable income. The stomach problems Spence incurred at Vicksburg had gotten better on a diet of good whole milk and Wanda's wonderful home cooking.

"He was a new man," Wanda said. "Having the money took the dread of life from Spence and he and I had some fine times together."

I think Wanda wanted to continue but she couldn't. Memories of her wonderful husband flooded her mind. He fought bravely for his country and suffered dreadfully during the siege of Vicksburg. He was a casualty of the war as much as the boys who died instantly in battle.

I remembered the stories Spence told and I thought of all the fine young men on both sides who died from illness after the war. Living conditions were deplorable at best during the war and many fine men succumbed to cholera, typhus, tuberculosis and many other diseases. It was one of the untold horrors of the war, yet to me these men were heroes just the same as the boys who rode bravely into enemy fire. I somehow hoped a grateful nation would remember these men.

Chapter 31

We enjoyed our visit with Wanda and promised to stop by again some day. We met with no mishaps on the trip. Jenny liked to drive the Ford. When we were on straight roads she was at ease behind the wheel. Curvy roads however caused her concern and on many occasions she would stop the vehicle and make me swap seats with her. The Ford handled beautifully on the rough roads and we were lucky enough to make the entire trip without having a single flat tire.

On entering Iuka we turned off the main road and drove the one block into the main downtown area. I could see Jenny smile as she looked at Swanson`s and all the other buildings around it that now belonged to our son. Any untrained observer could see immediately how successful these businesses were. Jenny reached and squeezed my hand. Throughout the years this had been her way of silently saying how much she loved me and how happy she was with our life together. I knew not to speak but my firm grip assured Jenny of my undying love for her.

Our grandchildren were both married. Laura Bell had a baby girl born on September the 12th, 1910. She was named after Jenny and everyone called her Jen. Laura Bell had been the first member of our family to go to college. She had attended the University of Mississippi at Oxford and had met and married Chet Farnsworth from Booneville. Chet agreed to open a branch of Swanson`s in Booneville. With Jed`s expert guidance, the store had already turned a nice profit in it`s second year of business.

Jed , Jr. married his childhood sweetheart, Joanna Crockett. Both were working at the stores on the town square. Neither Jed, Jr. or Joanna cared about college and were very happy living in Iuka.

As I looked at Jenny holding our great grand child in her lap, I felt a tear creep down my cheek. I don`t know why, but I thought of my childhood friend, Charley Rogers and all the other boys who had given their lives in the war. Why was I allowed to live so comfortably and have such a wonderful family when so many of my comrades and other boys from both north and south had given their lives for their country?

I didn't let the others see my tears as I quietly got up and strolled to the porch of the farm house. We decided years ago we would always spend Christmas together at the old home place. There was a special peace to the place particularly at Christmas. As I stood on the porch, I could almost feel the presence of Agnes by my side and feel her warm touch as she would always squeeze my hand before she retired each night. I realized what a tremendous influence my mother- in- law had been in my life and how much I admired her spirit and determination. I was a little ashamed for my feelings. Years ago I had forgotten my real mother and had loved and adored Agnes Swanson as if I had been born to her.

The night was pleasant but a slight chill was blowing from the north and I knew cold weather was on the way. Even though I grew up in Illinois I always hated the cold. I never seemed to be able to get warm when the north winds blew from December until March. Why, I don't know but I thought of the night we almost froze at Fort Donelson when we had discarded our heavy coats and the weather had changed so drastically. I thought of other soldiers having to deal with the cold in battlefields from Pennsylvania to Georgia. How terrible it must have been for the men in the prisons with barely enough food to eat and surely not enough warm clothing and cover.

Throughout the years I rarely thought of the war, but on this Christmas night of 1911 I could think of nothing else. I had talked to so many of the veterans of the war. Some of their stories were so horrible the mind couldn't believe these things actually occurred, but I knew they had, and I had run away from it. I always felt my life had accounted for something but I couldn't erase the fact I had been a coward and a deserter when my fellow comrades needed me. It didn't matter that I made up my mind I couldn't kill another human being. My place that day at Shiloh was with my friends and fellow soldiers from Illinois. I should have stayed and followed Lieutenant Ames and done what I could even if I had been killed.

As my mind was absorbed in these matters, I couldn't control myself. I ran to the barn and cried out loud. Sobs came from so deep inside me I felt my very soul was coming out of my body. I sat on the chest in the tack room where I had spent my first months living with Jenny and Agnes and finally my crying subsided. I was drained of all my strength, and there were no more tears left. I eased my head back on the saddle blanket I had used as a pillow so many times before and closed my eyes. I don't know how long I lay there, but I suddenly felt a gentle touch, and as I looked up, I saw Jenny looking down at me as she held my hand. She eased next to me, and we lay together without speaking for what must have been twenty minutes. Jenny had always been able to know my feelings and in her miraculous way she had known why I was so sorrowful. Finally Jenny broke the silence and spoke gently, but firmly.

"Marcus Wade, you are the finest man I will ever know. Inside the farm house is your loving family, and they wouldn't be who and what they are if it hadn't been for you. I don't give a hoot about what you did in Mr. Lincoln's Army. All I care about is that you came to Iuka and found me. Our lives together couldn't have been more perfect, and we wouldn't have had any of that if you were laying in a grave at Shiloh."

Jenny squeezed my arm and kissed me on the cheek. I turned and looked in her face and smiled. I knew that everything Jenny said was true. I stood on the floor of the tack room and hugged Jenny tightly.

"Let's go inside and enjoy our family," I said, as I led Jenny from the barn.

We decided to return to Memphis the day after New Year's. Our visit had been wonderful. We loved seeing the children and knew that some day we would permanently return to our home on the farm. Right now, however, Memphis and the river was somehow calling us. We had discussed with Jed and Molly our plans to go to Shiloh in April, and they agreed it was the right thing to do.

Weather was tolerable, and we arrived in Memphis by four in the afternoon. We had tragic news waiting on us as we arrived. Web Sanders had passed away four days after Christmas. His wife said he went to bed at his usual time and didn't wake up the next morning. The doctor said his heart must have given out. It was a devastating blow to us all but especially to me. Webster Sanders was the first colored man I had ever really gotten to know in my life, and he had become like a brother to me. He was without a doubt the kindest and most loving man I had ever known.

Stuart Moses, our trusting friend and manager of the first Ladies Home had taken over the arrangements while we were gone. She got permission from the Mayor for us to bury Web in a plot behind the home where he and his wife had served so faithfully. It was a rare gesture for the Mayor to make this concession for anyone, but for a colored man it was unheard of. The Mayor came to the funeral service, and I thanked him personally for allowing us this unusual privilege.

Webster's pastor led the service and all the ladies and children from both homes were there. Many members of the Providence Baptist Church where Web and Martha were members were in attendance. The weather was perfect for an early January day. There was just a hint of a breeze coming off the river and the temperature was at least fifty. The pastor did a beautiful job of describing Webster Sanders. As I looked out across the river moving swiftly below us, I thought of all the times Web and I had shared stories looking at the sunsets on the muddy water. I wasn't much of a Bible scholar but as I thought of my friend a portion of scripture came to my mind. It was somewhere in the New Testament and I think it was written by the Apostle Paul. I knew I didn't have it all exactly right but I tried to whisper it to myself.

"I have fought a good fight. I have finished my course. My Lord has laid up for me a crown of righteousness in his heavens."

I believed that at this moment my friend Webster Sanders was receiving his crown in heaven for a job well done.

6TH PENNSYLVANIA COLORED INFANTRY-- WILDERNESS CAMPAIGN
NORTHERN VIRGINIA---- JULY 1864- APRIL 1865

Web Sanders and his fellow infantrymen heard recent rumors that the war was almost over. General Robert E. Lee and his Army of Virginia had fought brilliantly and with such bravery that they earned the respect of all who met them in battle. The 6th Pennsylvania Colored Infantry spent most of the war in and around Washington guarding the Capitol City. On a few occasions they met Rebel soldiers in minor battles, mostly at supply compounds where the Southerners were trying to confiscate much needed food, clothing and ammunition. After Gettysburg and Vicksburg, President Lincoln's goal was the taking of Richmond and ending the war.

The 6th Pennsylvania was assigned to General Grant's forces under the direct command of Brigadier General Wade Hawthorne. Hawthorne followed with interest the progress made by colored troops. He came to the conclusion these men who had a special reason for winning the war could be counted on when the going got tougher and tougher. Hawthorne was not disappointed. The 6th Pennsylvania distinguished itself in all of the Wilderness Campaign, especially at Cold Harbor and Petersburg.

At Cold Harbor the Rebels had built heavy fortifications guarding the main access roads to Petersburg and Richmond. Fighting was fierce with heavy casualties on both sides. As he had done at Vicksburg, General Grant realized a frontal assault of the Rebel lines would bring total disaster to his forces. He decided to form a giant semi circle around the Confederates and continue bombardment until the Rebs depleted their supplies of food and ammunition. Most of the war had been fought in daylight, but at Cold Harbor night raids became common. The 6th Pennsylvania was particularly adept at pulling off these forays behind enemy lines. The dark skin of the men of 6th Pennsylvania made them almost impossible to see at night and their regular successes had become legendary among General Hawthorne's troops.

Corporal Webster Sanders led many such raids, and of the twenty two men under his command only one had been killed and two more wounded. Corporal Sanders and his men captured over eighty

Confederate rifles and numerous boxes of ammunition. On one such patrol the men under Corporal Sanders found the main coral where over sixty Rebel cavalry horses were kept. By keeping totally quiet the men were able to overcome the three guards and make off with the animals so vital to General Lee's depleted forces. General Hawthorne was so impressed by the work of Corporal Sanders and his men that he gave them all battle field citations and had a special letter sent to General Grant and President Lincoln telling of the exploits of this unusual unit. Web Sanders was promoted to the rank of Sergeant and was the first colored man to lead an entire company of his fellow Americans into battle without the direct leadership of a white officer. General Hawthorne said if he had to make a frontal assault on the heaviest fortified position on the Rebel line he would want to do it with Web Sanders at his side.

Web first noticed his heart racing on his return from a night raid at Cold Harbor. He had eaten some bacon and beans with his men and had two cups of strong coffee. As he and the men were swapping stories of the raid he had a strange sensation in his chest that alarmed him no end. His heart was beating very rapidly. He was feeling light headed. Not wanting to alarm his men he excused himself and retired to his tent where he immediately lay on his back. His heart was now pounding so hard his cot was shaking. His immediate reaction was that he was dying. He had been wounded twice and always thought of himself as a good physical specimen, but at this moment he had no control over what was happening inside his body. He became so weak he knew he couldn't make it to the surgeon's tent over one hundred yards away. He closed his eyes and decided if he was going to die, he would do it as comfortably as possible. Web didn't know how long he lay on the cot, but when he was almost asleep the fast heart beat suddenly stopped. He placed his hand to his throat and felt his pulse. The beating was back to normal. Web had no idea what had happened to him that night but at this moment he felt completely normal. He decided he wouldn't mention this event to anyone. He didn't want the men under his command to worry about him. Sergeant Sanders resumed his duties the next morning.

While the men were taking a break, Web and three of his fellow soldiers wandered through the group of horses they had taken from the Rebs two nights before. Web grabbed the mane of one of the

173

largest horses and swung himself up on the animal's back with great ease. All who witnessed this feat were amazed at the skill shown by Sergeant Sanders in the handling of the horse. It was obvious Web Sanders was no stranger to the backside of a horse. When questioned about it later, Sergeant Sanders said when he had been in the orphanage in Philadelphia the head master had a horse and Web, being the oldest boy in the home, was allowed to care for the animal. Web learned everything there was to know about a horse. By the time he was fourteen, he was an expert rider, with or without a saddle.

One of the brigade officers, Lieutenant Marion Winkler, observed Web Sanders' exploits on the horse and informed Colonel David Henson there was an expert horseman among the colored troops. Badly needing riders for night raids farther inside enemy lines, Colonel Henson immediately informed Sergeant Sanders he was being transferred to Lieutenant Winkler's light cavalry. He would lead a raid tonight on the giant Rebel ammunition dump at Petersburg. General Grant sent word the war could be shortened by several months if somehow the Confederate's main ammunition supply could be destroyed. Web Sanders was elated! He had always wanted to be a cavalryman, but to this point colored soldiers had not been allowed to ride army horses in battle.

A plan was devised. Six well armed men would follow Sergeant Sanders through the back roads and wooded areas. They would sneak behind enemy lines and attempt the destruction of the Rebel ammunition supply depot just outside Petersburg.

Maps were shown to the men of the entire area, and by the time the small force left camp Web Sanders knew exactly where he was going and what his job would be once he got there. One of the men in the group was an ordinance specialist. He took large amounts of gunpowder, and by encasing the powder in heavy burlap bags, made a powerful explosive device. It was estimated if the powder could be detonated at the ammunition dump, a large portion of the arms and ammunition would be destroyed in one giant explosion.

The decision was made to go as late as possible and still get the job done before daylight. Officers on both sides tended to relax their picket lines after midnight, and it was hoped there would only be a small contingent of Rebs guarding the dump when Web and his men arrived around two in the morning.

The plan worked to perfection.   Web was so skillful in his horsemanship that the seven riders were within twenty yards of the entrance to the dump before Web had them stop and dismount. Colonel Henson told the men on this raid Sergeant Sanders would be in total command and his orders were to be followed without question.   The other men, all white soldiers, were so impressed with Web Sanders and his skills they gladly did what he said.

Web sent two men ahead to dispose of the only two guards at the entrance to the supply dump. Not a shot was fired as the two veteran Union soldiers easily killed the two guards with bayonets.   The startled guards never saw or heard their assailants until they were falling dead to the ground. Web then led Lieutenant Marshall, the explosive expert, inside the giant enclosure.   Several bags of explosives were carefully placed, and after lighting fuses timed to detonate in five minutes, Lieutenant Marshall and Web ran from the enclosure.

It took the group about four minutes to get back to their horses, mount, and make a hasty retreat away from the expected blast. When the first bags of powder exploded, they evidently set off kegs of Confederate powder. The next blast was so loud and fierce that the ground shook for a mile in all directions. The entire supply depot was destroyed in less than two minutes.   Web and his men couldn't believe the sheer size of the blast. The results were far greater than any had expected.

Sergeant Sanders became an instant hero to the men of General Hawthorne's Brigade. He was invited to sit in the officers tent and discuss different battles. On more than one occasion he was asked for advice from his superior officers.

Before the war ended, Sergeant Sanders experienced three more episodes of rapid heart beat, but in all cases the heart returned to normal after a short time. Sergeant Sanders would be decorated three times for bravery in action. He was considered one of the finest soldiers in Grant's Army, colored or white.

After the Petersburg raid, General Grant ordered an attack on all main Confederate positions. On April 2nd Petersburg fell to the superior Union forces.   One of Lee's most able and trusted subordinates, General A.P. Hill, was killed. Richmond was evacuated and on April 9th General Lee surrendered his army to General Grant at Appomattox Courthouse. The war that had started at Fort Sumter in 1861 was finally over.

Web Sanders would continue his service to his country by joining General Phil Sheridan in fighting to secure the west from hostile Indians.

He never mentioned his heart condition to anyone, yet he knew that some day this strange malady would take his life.

Chapter 32

The day of Web's funeral his wife, Martha, handed me an envelope. She said Web had instructed her to give it to me if anything happened to him. I sat down on the concrete bench behind the Ladies Home and started reading.

"Marcus,

I been experiencing a little discomfort lately and I fear my old heart condition has finally caught up with me. I didn't tell you about it but I have had some problems since the war. At first my spells didn't have any pain with them but lately I have had some pretty tough nights. I finally shared my problem with Martha and she wanted me to go to Doctor Roberts. I guess I should do it but I have a feeling my days are numbered and I needed to tell you something I couldn't tell you face to face. I love you, Marcus. You is the first white man who ever took me for what I was and I appreciate that more than you know. When I looks back at that day I walked up to the home for the ladies I know now that I was led there as surely as if I had a rope around my neck. I didn't tell you, but I had asked for work for over two hours at all the stores and houses on the river front. I was turned away from them all and many of the folk wouldn't even talk to me. I was about to turn and go back to the river and try to beg for enough money for supper. I was down to my last fifty cents.

You probably don't remember it but you must have been working on that loose board on the front steps when your foot fell through the rotten timber. I don't know for sure what you said but I heard it from a block away. Something told me to go up to you and ask for work. Well, I guess you might say the rest is history.

I have loved every minute with you and Miss Jenny and all the ladies. I has been cared for like family and made to feel needed. Me and Martha has tried our best to do right with you all. It is you, Marcus, more than anyone else who has been the real reason for my happiness. Our times together has been the best times of my life. I want you to know you are something special.

177

I appreciate you finally sharing with me about Mr. Lincoln's Gold. I don't know of any other man on earth who would do what you and Miss Jenny has done with all that money. I has a good feeling that God will bless you because of it.

I had a real bad night on Tuesday and I feel the next spell might be my last. I had to let you know, Marcus, that I'll miss you most of all. We weren't born the same color but you is my brother and I looks forward to seeing you again in Glory. Thank you again for saving my life and being my friend.

Web"

I was sobbing so hard I could hardly fold the letter and put it back in the envelope. Why hadn't I told Web how much his friendship meant to me? Surely he knew I shared his feelings. I knew at that moment I would never let another person read this special letter from my deceased friend. This was between Web and me and I would keep the letter and cherish it always. I thought how eloquent Wester Sanders was. He made a few errors of grammar and his writing was a little hard to read in places, but few learned white men could have written better.

The wind off the river had freshened and I walked to the Ford and drove home. Jenny could tell I had been crying and she simply pulled me close and let me know she would always be there for me. I needed her comfort this night. I had lost my closest friend and I knew I would never have another who could replace him.

For a while I visited Web's grave daily. Usually I would just sit and look at the nice marble head stone the ladies had placed on his final resting place. The words described Web pretty well.

WEBSTER SANDERS
Mar. 8, 1842—Dec. 28, 1911
Loving- Faithful- Honest-Caring
Trustworthy - Diligent- Courteous
Hard working
A REAL MAN AMONG MEN

On a few occasions, I would catch myself talking to Web as if I expected him to answer. I finally stopped going to the grave every day. I would usually stop by after church on Sunday to check on the condition of the grass and make sure the area was clean. I told the custodian at the Ladies Home he didn't need to check on Mr. Sander's grave. I planned to care for it as long as I was able. I felt this was the least I could do for my trusted friend.

I recalled the last conversation I had with Web. We were sitting on our favorite bench by the river watching some of the fishermen check their lines.

" Marcus, you has got to be the most unusual veteran that fought in the war. Why, you could sell your story to one of them big northern magazines for an awful lot of money. When I think of you riding lickety split down that road at Shiloh I has got to laugh a little. Of all the wagons at Shiloh that day you just happens to end up in the one that had all of Mr. Lincoln's Gold in it."

I remember looking at Web, and we both laughed out loud! There really was something funny about it after all. Men were dying all around me, and yet I was towing a half million dollars behind me, and no one bothered to so much as holler at me.

"You know I can never tell anyone about that day, Web," I said as I turned to look my friend in the eyes. "Why, who in the world would believe I didn't know the gold was back there and that we have used so much of it to help others."

"I know, Marcus," said Web. "I just think it's the best story I ever heard. I just wish I could tell everybody about it. Don't you worry none though. I ain't told Martha that you was in Mr. Lincoln's army and I sure ain't told about the gold."

When I first told Web about my past I had not mentioned the gold but as we became so close I shared this with him also. He never so much as asked me for one Gold Eagle. Web accepted my story as fact and praised me for the way Jenny and I had handled the situation.

I missed my dear friend but realized he had lived a good long life and not only fought for his country but was a true hero. Few men could live up to the words Stuart and the other ladies had put on the tombstone, but former Sergeant Webster Sanders could. I was thankful to have known him. He really was a 'man among men'.

February was brutal in Memphis. We had one heavy snow and an ice storm that caused a lot of tree limbs to fall. The streets got so slick we couldn't drive the Ford without sliding off the road. Jenny and I had plenty of firewood stacked behind the house. We enjoyed the comfort of our home during the hard winter days. Stella would come over from next door and she and Jenny would sit in front of the fire and gossip. I became a real fan of the Memphis Appeal and read every word of the paper each day. I knew nothing of the world across the oceans and always read with interest the articles about India, China, France, Spain and all the other places of the world. I had been a fair student in school but back at Galena we rarely studied about foreign countries. I figure, Mrs. Harris, our teacher didn't know too much about them either, and that's why she didn't try to teach us about them. I was hungry for knowledge about the world and read everything I could.

Jenny had become quite adept at crocheting. She could make place mats, arm covers for our chairs, napkins and even bed spreads. It passed the time for her, and I could tell she was quite proud of her results.

I never tired of Jenny's company. I had my friends at the store down the street and the men in my Sunday School class, but Jenny was my closest friend. We had always been affectionate to each other, and we still had our special ways of showing that affection. On more than one occasion we would go to the Peabody Hotel, eat a fine meal in the Plantation Ball Room and then retire to a room we had rented. It was an extravagance, but we felt the $6.00 we spent on the room was worth it. There was a naughty feeling about making love in a hotel room, and even at our age we both still cherished those moments.

By mid March the weather turned for the better. We started making our plans for the trip to Shiloh in early April.

We decided to stay at the farm in Iuka. Although a lot of the roads in rural Mississippi were not yet prepared for the automobile, there was a route through Corinth and then north to Shiloh that was passable if we could avoid heavy rains. We could travel about thirty five miles an hour so the trip to Shiloh would take less than two hours from the farm.

The schedule of events for the celebration at Shiloh was listed in all the local papers. April 5th was on a Sunday so they decided to have the main ceremonies on Monday the 6th. There was to be a flag raising ceremony at the Shiloh National Cemetery at 11:A.M. and speeches by several dignitaries. Colonel Jordan, an aide to Grant in 1862 would represent the north and Major Scranton of General Albert Sydney Johnston's staff would speak for the south. These men would be well into their eighties by now.

President of the United States, William Howard Taft, was sending his Vice President, James Schoolcraft Sherman, to speak on his behalf.

After the main ceremony at the cemetery, there was to be a picnic on the bluff overlooking the Tennessee River. Special guests would be all the men in attendance who had participated in the battle.

There was to be separate smaller gatherings throughout the afternoon at the various monuments located throughout the park honoring the various states. I noticed with interest that Governor Bates of Illinois would be at the new Illinois Monument when it was to be unveiled at three o'clock, Monday afternoon.

Chapter 33

We got up very early on Monday morning April 6th. We had little difficulty on our journey up to Pittsburg Landing. We arrived at the headquarters building around nine and were amazed at the sheer numbers of people milling about. Many of the veterans of the battle were dressed in their uniforms and were walking through the cemetery looking at the grave sites. Jenny remarked that she thought there were more Confederate veterans in attendance than Yankees. I feel sure that, somehow, through the intervening years these men had purchased or had their wives make them new uniforms. All were spotless and showed no wear whatsoever. None of the sleek uniforms I saw this day would have been on the young soldiers back in 1862.

We parked the Ford in the designated area provided and joined the crowds looking at the graves and the items inside the headquarters building. There was a large map on one of the walls of the main building showing the location of all the units from both sides during both days of the battle. It took me several minutes to locate on the map the 22nd Illinois Regulars under Colonel Rogers, but finally, I found it near the old Shiloh Church. The location changed on the 6th when the Rebs had driven our unit over near the river. I found where our Illinois boys were around General Sherman's position on the morning of the 7th and by evening had been one of the main units to force the Rebs into a full retreat. I had trained and lived with these boys for months and seeing their accomplishments here in this great battle made me feel a little proud. I was now a southerner and my children and grand children were all born Mississippian's. I had been born in Illinois, and although I never wanted to fight in the war, I still had a feeling of pride in my heritage and in the land where I had been raised.

Inside the main hall were weapons of all descriptions. We inspected various uniforms, tents, pots and pans, and many other items taken from the field of battle here at Shiloh.

I told Jenny I wanted to walk over to the old Shiloh Church and see if I could find the place where Charley fell and where I confiscated the wagon containing Mr. Lincoln's Gold.

It was a little farther to the church than I thought and it must have taken us fifteen minutes to get there. On the way, we passed the pond where boys from both sides had come to wash their wounds. The little pond had a sign by it and would always be known as "Bloody Pond." Jenny grabbed my arm and squeezed it tightly. As she stared at the waters of the pond, it was if she could actually see the boys in their agony washing their wounds in the cool water.

The little church had changed very little from that terrible morning when Charley went inside to look around. A nice sign had been placed at the entrance by the Park Commission explaining how the battle got it's name from the small church. The road looked slightly different, but as I gazed south from the porch of the church I could see where Charley had been struck and killed. I saw the large overhanging tree with missing bottom branches. They had been blown off and hit the two men driving the money wagon. As I stood looking at my past, I could feel sweat beading up on my brow. I was being transported back fifty years to the day I witnessed Hell on earth. I heard Charley's scream. I saw boys falling to their deaths dressed only in their pants and long john tops. I saw shells bursting all around me driving my comrades toward the river. I could hear the yells of men on both sides as the hordes of charging Rebels moved relentlessly forward. I kept waiting for the shell to hit that would take me out of my misery and let me die with honor, next to Charley.

After what seemed like hours, but was actually only a few minutes, I heard Jenny,

"Marcus. Oh, Marcus my darling. It's all right. Everything is quiet and peaceful. Come, sweetheart hold me."

I turned slowly to Jenny and suddenly it was 1911 again and I was all right. Jenny was by my side, and I heard birds in the trees calling their mates. I gathered my dear wife in my arms and hugged her tightly. She was my comfort, my strength, the love of my life. She was the reason I lived, and as I held her in my arms, I said a silent prayer thanking God for her.

I looked at my watch and told Jenny we needed to walk back toward the headquarters for the ceremonies. We arrived just in time to get two of the last available seats in front of the podium.

Vice President Sherman was the first to speak. He appeared to me to be in his mid fifties. He was a little chubby but nice looking. He wore wire rimmed glasses and spoke with a crisp northern brogue. I saw in the program where the Vice President was a New Yorker. I thought it commendable that the man who held the second highest office in our land would take the time to come to Tennessee to help honor the men who fought in a battle fifty years before. He got the immediate attention of the entire crowd with his first words:

"As we peer out at the smooth waters of the beautiful Tennessee River flowing quietly below us it is hard to imagine that on April 6th and 7th of 1862 the bitterest battle that had yet been fought on the North American Continent was fought here between the North and the South in what we now know as the Battle of Shiloh."

The Vice President paused momentarily, took off his wire rimmed glasses, wiped them with his handkerchief, placed them back on his nose and continued,

"Men from both sides were meeting in their first great battle of the war and fought with extreme bravery and fierce determination. Each man felt that the cause for what he fought that day was just and that his part in the struggle was important and vital to the outcome of the war."

Vice President Sherman raised his handkerchief to his mouth and coughed quietly. He paused, looked again at the river and said.

"Before Shiloh, people on both sides felt the war would be over in a matter of months. After the battle here the people of America knew the great war would last for many days to come. The resolve of the people of the south was strong, and Shiloh proved they were willing to die for their cause. So was the case of the men in blue as over thirteen thousand brave Union soldiers gave their lives in the two day struggle. General Grant would make a name for himself here and go on to become the most revered officer of the war, later even being elected as our nations president."

The Vice President took a sip of water from a glass on the podium. He continued.

"The South would lose one of it's ablest leaders as General Albert Sydney Johnston was struck down on the first day of battle. Over ten thousand southerners would die in the fierce fighting."

The Vice President moved away from the podium and seemed to lose himself in the moment. He looked in all directions at the vast battle field as if he could see the carnage that occurred on the very spot where he was standing. He composed himself and walked back to the speakers platform.

"Today, as we commemorate the fiftieth anniversary of the Battle of Shiloh, we proclaim that never again will the noise of battle be heard on these hallowed grounds. The fields of Shiloh will remain silent as a tribute to the over twenty thousand Americans who gave their lives here.

We have in our midst this morning several hundred of the men who fought so bravely on these rolling fields. They are our distinguished and honored guests, and it is with the highest esteem that we recognize them at this time. Would you men of both the Blue and the Gray please stand and let us salute you."

As the men from both Armies started to rise, shouts and applause started to ripple throughout the more than three thousand in attendance. By the time the old soldiers were on their feet, the applause was deafening. As we looked at all the veterans of the battle, we could see tears streaming down many of their faces. Men who had been mortal enemies in battle were now standing together, some even shaking hands as their families and friends saluted them. I looked at Jenny. She was crying openly while clapping as hard as she could.

As I thought of my own memories of that fateful day, I realized each of the men here had their own story of the battle. Many had been wounded and all had lost friends or possibly brothers in the fighting. Not a single man here was the same after Shiloh. They may have experienced more fierce battles in the war but the struggle on this bluff over the river will be forever implanted in their minds as their first taste of the Hell of war.

The applause lasted for at least five minutes. After the men sat back down, the Vice President said a few more words and then gave way to the other speakers of the day.

The Governor of the State of Tennessee gave a stirring tribute to the men and the program closed with a few remarks by the two veterans representing their respective armies. I thought they did a commendable job and was particularly impressed by the statements made by Colonel Winston Jordan who had been with Grant when the fighting started. He was probably in his late seventies or early eighties, but Colonel Jordan was quite spry and eloquent.

"I remember the morning was calm and serene. I had carried the General's coffee to him as I did most mornings, so we could discuss the orders for the day. The General planned to give the men a couple of hours to enjoy breakfast and take a stroll around the countryside before having inspection and drills. The weather was very pleasant. There was a nice breeze blowing off the river and the sun was creeping through the trunks of the trees on the bluff. General Grant was in good spirits and mentioned the high morale of the men and how pleased he was that our move toward Corinth was progressing so well."

The Colonel's voice wasn't forceful but strong enough to be heard by all in the audience. He took a sip of water before he continued.

"I heard the first report of cannon fire and looked at the General who stood to his feet. We both assumed that some of our batteries were testing their guns. We were located just north of where we are standing now and the battle started several hundred yards to the west in that direction."

Colonel Jordan pointed to the west and looked at the horizon as if he expected to see the Rebels charging through the woods. He continued.

"Lieutenant Scoggins, from Sherman's corps, came galloping into camp and raced to our tent. He shouted that the Rebs were attacking in full force and several of our encampments had been overrun. General Grant told me to get all the staff officers assembled at once and to see that a defensive perimeter be set up around the command post."

Colonel Jordan continued to tell of the actions taken and how serious the position of General Grant and his men were in the first hours of the battle.

"At one point," said the Colonel. "We thought of sending General Grant to the boats and having him retire to Savannah. The outcome of the battle was in doubt, and we knew the death or capture of General Grant would be a severe blow to our cause."

Colonel Jordan told of the battle turning late in the day and the lessening of pressure from the Confederates.

"We didn't know Sydney Johnston had been killed and we thought the Rebs had just tired and fallen back to regroup. We found out the next morning about General Johnston's death and realized we had been given a reprieve. With the arrival of Buell during the night, the advantage was ours and the southern boys were no match for what Grant threw at them on the second morning."

I thought I saw a few tears in the old Colonel's eyes as he concluded.

"I can only say that I have the upmost respect and admiration for the boys in gray who fought us here on this bluff. Never before in history have men given more than these men gave for their field commanders. They didn't lose this battle, they were simply overwhelmed by superior numbers and equipment."

Colonel Jordan wiped his eyes and finished his speech.

"I would like to close by paying tribute to all you brave men from both sides who have returned here today. The world would never be the same after Shiloh and you were all a part of it."

The Colonel had summed it up pretty well. Major Scranton of the south did an equally admirable job and also commended his opponents in the great battle.

We all sang America the Beautiful, and the young pastor of the still active Shiloh Baptist Church closed the program with a short prayer.

Dinner was provided by volunteer workers from nearby towns. The ham sandwiches were adequate and I thought the lemonade and tea cookies were especially good.

After lunch Jenny and I picked up a few souvenirs from the gift center, and I got a copy of President Lincoln's Gettysburg Address. I had read it once years ago in the Memphis Appeal but wanted a copy for myself.

We arrived at the Illinois Monument in time to view it before Governor Bates started the ceremony. The monument was indeed impressive. It seemed to me that the Illinois monument was the largest we saw during our inspection of the grounds. The marble statue depicted three Union soldiers in full battle gear with a large statue of a lady standing above them. The lady wore a robe that was stretched out as if to cover the men from harm. I don't know if the lady was supposed to be an angel or maybe a mother protecting her children. Whatever it was, it caught the eye and made you feel like you were truly standing in a holy place.

I wasn't prepared for what we found on the back side of the monument. The names of all the men killed or missing from Illinois were carved on the back of the monument. The list was enormous. It started with Jacob Abrams at the top and finished with Simon Zinn. We tried to estimate the number of names. It was almost impossible. There had to be at least seven to eight thousand. As we scanned those killed we saw Charley Rogers' name. Listed just above Charley was Billy Perkins who shared our tent at Savannah. I hadn't seen Billy on the morning the battle started, so I didn't know his fate.

As we got to the list of the missing, my heart sank as I came to my own name, Marcus Wade. I don't know why, but I figured I would have just been forgotten. I realized since I was an official casualty of the war, my relatives back in Galena would have been notified. I doubt my daddy would have cared at all, but I feel my mother, and probably my grandparents, would have been saddened by the news. I knew that by now they would all be dead and my secret life would never be known to them.

Jenny squeezed my hand. For some reason I became nervous. There were several of the Illinois veterans there at the monument, and I realized I could be standing next to one of my former comrades. I had to hope the fifty years that had passed would keep any one from recognizing me. I never had a weight problem and I still had all my hair, although it had turned slightly gray. Jenny said I didn't look a lot different from the nineteen year old who entered Swanson's store that April morning back in 1862.

We completed our circle of the huge monument and ended up back at the front where Governor Richard Bates was beginning his walk up the many steps of the monument. Wooden benches had been brought in, and we found a seat next to a veteran in uniform and I assume his wife. I looked closely at the man but saw no resemblance to anyone I had known when I was in Mr. Lincoln's Army.

I must say the monument before us was impressive. I was surprised this magnificent edifice could have been built for $150,000. I felt good that we had used the last of Mr. Lincoln's Gold to help pay for this tribute to the men from Illinois who had fought and died here.

Governor Bates didn't talk very long, but I thought what he said was appropriate and to the point. Jenny tightened her grip on my arm when the Governor thanked the anonymous donor who paid for most of the cost to construct the monument. Since Mr. Lincoln was also from Illinois, I figured he would be pleased to have had a major part in the event.

Chapter 34

I was relieved and happy we had attended the festivities at Shiloh. It was a strange feeling actually being back on the battlefield. I looked at the peace and quiet of the place, and knew we had done the right thing in coming. As we walked back toward the parking lot, we passed by a long mound under large oak trees. The sign on the mound stated this place had been a trench where Rebel soldiers were buried together. The place had never been disturbed. There was no way to know how many southern boys were in the mass grave.

We talked to one of the Park Rangers and he said there were three such graves on the battlefield. It was estimated at least five thousand Confederate soldiers were still entombed under these large mounds of earth.

He told us there had been two such Union graves after the battle. During the intervening years, the bodies had been removed from the mass graves and were now buried in the huge cemetery by the river.

I think Jenny was overwhelmed by what she had seen this day. She had been a part of the Battle of Iuka and had seen her share of death. She heard the stories of all the returning veterans but actually being on this vast battlefield and seeing what occurred here was more than she could comprehend. I knew from this day forward Jenny would have a different view of the war and what the men on both sides endured.

We took another look at the cemetery and looked down at the river one last time. We strolled to the embankment just above Pittsburg Landing, and I showed Jenny where the gunboats had unloaded back in 1862. We eventually found Charley's grave. I was pleased to know he was there with other boys from home.

We picked up the Ford at the parking area and started south to the exit of the park. As we drove past the Peach Orchard we were reminded of what the curator said about the day the bullets were in such great number that all the blossoms had been blown from the trees. The ground looked as if there had been a pink snow during the day. Before we left the entrance, we looked to the west and saw the now infamous Hornet's Nest. The boys in Grant's Corps had given the name to this thick wooded area because the sounds of all the bullets going through the branches sounded like hornets in flight. Cannons in perfect order were in several spots pointing toward the river. The guns left no doubt in the visitor's minds that they were standing on hallowed ground.

As we got to the main gate of the park, we stopped and thanked the nice attendant for the courtesy shown us and for the way in which the Park Commission had prepared and now cared for the battlefield. It was eerie but quite beautiful.

I turned back and looked over the battlefield and realized I would never return to this place again. I had been here twice in my life, and that was enough. I was glad to have been a part in the building of the Illinois Monument but I had no desire to ever come back here. This was a part of my past, and I was going home and enjoy my family and look to the future. Jenny and I had decided to sell our place in Memphis and retire to the farm. We weren't getting any younger, and we wanted to spend our last days with our children, grandchildren and now one great grandchild.

I thought of all the people we had helped with Mr. Lincoln's Gold and wondered what had happened in their lives because of it. I thought of the Ladies Homes in Memphis and all the good that had come from that venture.

For some reason I thought of Mr. Lincoln. From all I had read of President Lincoln I felt he was a fine man. He had been placed in a situation he hadn't asked for and had somehow brought this country back together. I turned to Jenny and asked her to read me the Gettysburg Address we purchased back at the gift shop. Jenny smiled and opened the envelope and started reading.

"Four score and seven years ago our fathers brought forth on this continent a new nation, conceived in liberty and dedicated to the proposition that all men are created equal."

As Jenny read these stirring words written and spoken by President Lincoln, I thought of my dear friend Webster Sanders. Because he was colored, he had never been treated the same as men his same age who were white. The only way Web gained equality with his peers was his uncanny abilities in battle. Web and hundreds like him would never be accepted as equals in this country, both in the north and the south. As a child growing up in Galena, I had always been taught that colored people were inferior to whites and we shouldn't have anything to do with them. President Lincoln said that 'all men are created equal.' Had the war really changed that? I guess some things changed for the better, but I doubted a colored man was much better off today than he was before the war. All the colored men I met in Memphis were porters, waiters, bell hops or common laborers. They were indeed free men, but were they really equal to the ones of us who had been lucky enough to have been born to white parents? Would time change this? I knew it would not happen in my lifetime. I also knew it wasn't just a southern thing. Web Sanders had told of relatives in Pennsylvania who were no better off today than they were before the war. In Memphis and Iuka colored people had their own churches, schools and even funeral homes. When we buried Web behind the Ladies Home, a colored mortuary handled all the arrangements. Web Sanders was the best friend I ever had, but I will admit that I always looked at him as a colored man, not just a man. I knew he was kind and gentle and would do anything for me. Although I wouldn't admit it, I always placed myself above him simply because I was white and he was colored.

I knew my grandchildren would never go to school or church with colored children so what had all the killing really accomplished. Was it worth it for so many fine men from both sides to be slaughtered like cattle? I guess some good came from the war, but to my mind it was folly. Had we learned our lesson that would keep Americans from ever fighting Americans again in war? I had to hope so.

I thought again of Mr. Lincoln's Gold. I knew it made a tremendous difference in our lives. Agnes could never have re-stocked the store. We couldn't have given so many jobs to all the boys who returned from the war. We would never have been able to help all the churches and individual families to a better life.

Of all the men Jenny, Agnes and I had known of who had fought in the war, I thought first of Jedediah Tomkins and the young man Albert, from Michigan. I always felt these two young boys epitomized what had been wrong with the war. Here were two boys the same age, the same color and with the same desires in life who had been killed in fighting among themselves. As I continued to drive south toward home, I could only hope the boys who survived the war found a better life waiting for them when they got home.

Jenny continued reading The Gettysburg Address and came to the last section.

"That we here highly resolve that these dead shall not have died in vain, that this nation shall have a new birth of freedom and that this government of the people, by the people, for the people shall not perish from the earth."

Jenny slid over next to me and put her head on my shoulder. I kissed her on the top of her head.

"You know, honey. Mr. Lincoln must have been some special person." I said. "It's a shame some idiot had to kill him. I think we would have been a lot better off if he had lived."

I thought of what Mr. Lincoln's Gold would have been used for if I hadn't run off with it. I knew it probably wouldn't have made any difference in the war or really anything else. I am sure the boys in General Grant's Army got their back pay before too many weeks passed. The Federal Government didn't go bankrupt just because I took a little of their money. Knowing what I knew now of Mr. Lincoln, I think if I could sit down and tell him all the wonderful stories of how his gold had been used he would have been pleased. I would like to think so.

We arrived back in Iuka before dark and Jenny cooked us a hot skillet of corn bread. We sat in front of the fireplace and had cornbread and milk. This had always been one of my favorites, and the hot cornbread was particularly good this night. Jenny and I talked of Memphis and our friends and how much we had enjoyed our years there. We knew that somehow God had sent us there to do the work we had done with the Agnes Swanson Ladies Homes. We really liked Memphis, but as we sat in our living room at the farm this quiet April night, we knew we were back where we belonged. This was where our lives together started and, God willing, this is where we would have many more good days.

Jenny cleaned up the kitchen and we retired to our bedroom. It had been a long day and we were both tired. As we got in bed Jenny slid over beside me and put her arms around me and said,

"I love you, Marcus Wade. I love the little boy from Illinois. I love the soldier in Mr. Lincoln's Army. I love the man who brought happiness to this house and fathered our sweet son. I wouldn't swap you for all the men in either of the armies who fought in the stupid war. Don't ever leave me, Marcus."

I wrapped my arms tightly around my sweet Jenny and we held each other until I heard her smooth breathing that told me she had fallen asleep.

My mind wandered to many things.

Had I somehow been chosen by a higher power for something special in life? I know I tried as hard as I could to do the right things with Mr. Lincoln's Gold. I can truthfully say I never wanted to use any of the money for our personal gain. Was this why my life had been so perfect? Had God sent me into Swanson's that morning in 1862 so I would find Jenny? Was God blessing us now because of our faithfulness?

I wasn't sure the answers to these questions. One thing I did know for sure, however. I wouldn't trade places with any man on the face of this earth.

About The Author

Mr. Caldwell is an honor graduate of the University of Mississippi with majors in English and History. He retired from his successful antique business in 1998. He is active in his local church where he has served as a Deacon and has taught an adult Sunday School class for over twenty years. Mr. Caldwell is heavily involved in local civic affairs including Kiwanis, Methodist Senior Services Retirement Community and the Tupelo City Museum.

Mr. Caldwell and his wife live in the home they built in 1955. They have three sons and four grandchildren. He likes to play golf, fish and write.

Mr. Caldwell is an avid history buff. He has visited all the battlefields mentioned in his book.